‖‖‖‖‖‖‖‖‖
✓ **W9-ARX-802**

"Why do you hate me so much?" Eden asked quietly.

Lang flashed her a brilliant look. "Don't be ridiculous. I don't hate you at all."

"But you find no joy in my sudden entry into your life?"

"Maybe I'm hurting too much," he said involuntarily, but it was too late to recall those revealing words.

"Are you trying to make me feel more guilty?"

"Are you? Marvelous," he mocked. "How come you lied so easily? How come you couldn't even warn me?"

"I told you. I couldn't go against Dad. I know it was wrong, but why are you being so hard on me? Is it me, or do you distrust all women?"

"Not until I met you."

BOOK EXCHANGE
(843) 556-5051
1219 SAVANNAH HWY.
CHARLESTON, SC 29407

Margaret Way takes great pleasure in her work and works hard at her pleasure. She enjoys tearing off to the beach with her family at weekends, loves haunting galleries and auctions and is completely given over to French champagne "for every possible joyous occasion." She was born and educated in the river city of Brisbane, Australia, and now lives within sight and sound of beautiful Moreton Bay.

Look out in December for
Outback Angel by Margaret Way (#3727)

Books by Margaret Way

Don't miss any of our special offers. Write to us at the following address for information on our newest releases.

Harlequin Reader Service
U.S.: 3010 Walden Ave., P.O. Box 1325, Buffalo, NY 14269
Canadian: P.O. Box 609, Fort Erie, Ont. L2A 5X3

MARGARET WAY

Mistaken Mistress

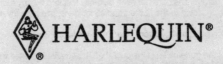

TORONTO • NEW YORK • LONDON
AMSTERDAM • PARIS • SYDNEY • HAMBURG
STOCKHOLM • ATHENS • TOKYO • MILAN • MADRID
PRAGUE • WARSAW • BUDAPEST • AUCKLAND

If you purchased this book without a cover you should be aware that this book is stolen property. It was reported as "unsold and destroyed" to the publisher, and neither the author nor the publisher has received any payment for this "stripped book."

ISBN 0-373-03715-5

MISTAKEN MISTRESS

First North American Publication 2002.

Copyright © 2002 by Margaret Way, Pty., Ltd.

All rights reserved. Except for use in any review, the reproduction or utilization of this work in whole or in part in any form by any electronic, mechanical or other means, now known or hereafter invented, including xerography, photocopying and recording, or in any information storage or retrieval system, is forbidden without the written permission of the publisher, Harlequin Enterprises Limited, 225 Duncan Mill Road, Don Mills, Ontario, Canada M3B 3K9.

All characters in this book have no existence outside the imagination of the author and have no relation whatsoever to anyone bearing the same name or names. They are not even distantly inspired by any individual known or unknown to the author, and all incidents are pure invention.

This edition published by arrangement with Harlequin Books S.A.

® and TM are trademarks of the publisher. Trademarks indicated with ® are registered in the United States Patent and Trademark Office, the Canadian Trade Marks Office and in other countries.

Visit us at www.eHarlequin.com

Printed in U.S.A.

PROLOGUE

FOR over twenty years Owen Carter had tried to forget he had a daughter. Not that he had seen her, not for a second. Not until this day of sorrows; of leaden skies and driving rain. He had journeyed over a thousand miles to sit in the back pew of a lovely old stone church never free of the unshakeable bond that tied him to Cassandra. Her tragic death at the age of forty-three had never been foreseen, now tormented by his memories, he attended her funeral, staring longingly into a face so like Cassandra's the pull to go to the young woman was enormous. He almost sprang up, but he didn't dare. Not *now*.

His daughter was his beautiful Cassandra all over again. The same silky black cloud of hair, the same extraordinary eyes, iris-blue, violet, purple. In Cassandra it had depended on the clothes she wore and the intensity of her moods. On this tragic day, tears starting down her cheeks as she followed her mother's flower-decked casket, his daughter's eyes were almost navy, the very white skin, which contrasted so strikingly with her hair, as pale as milk. They had never met but he would have known her anywhere.

It was Cassandra, come back to him.

His eyes so riveted to his daughter, must somehow have broken through her miasma of grief. She turned her head abruptly as if she felt his look, fully focusing on him. It was a deep, direct look so much like Cassandra's a slight keening broke from him and his broad shoulders crumpled like someone had delivered a king hit to his solar plexus. His daughter. My God! The great love, so deeply rooted in his heart it never saw the sun, suddenly sprang into frantic bloom. Nothing would stop it.

5

Surely the gods had punished him enough? He had cloistered both of them in his heart, Cassandra and Eden, thinking in some tortured way he'd been protecting the child. Now that was all over as the dynamic force that was in him rose to the challenge. She's mine, he thought triumphantly. My own flesh and blood. My daughter. The daughter denied me.

Hear me, Cassandra, he cried silently, channelling his thought to the lily draped casket.

This is my daughter. I've come to take her home.

CHAPTER ONE

LANG and Owen left the meeting together.

"That went well," Lang remarked with satisfaction, moving through the lunchtime crowd with such smooth confidence people found themselves quite happy to go around him.

"If it did it was thanks to you," Owen admitted with open affection. "I thought I was a tough negotiator but you've overtaken me. Nowadays you're the key player."

"But isn't that the way you want it?" Lang glanced sideways at his partner's face. Although Owen looked as fit as ever, indeed he looked what he was, a handsome highly successful man in his prime, the old punch was gone. For the past six months it seemed Owen was no longer driven by his vast business interests. Somehow he had removed himself from his life in the fast track, his focus clearly elsewhere.

It was odd. Perturbing. As were the monthly trips to the state capital Brisbane, the reasons for which Owen had never divulged. Not that he had to. Owen Carter answered to no one. Not him, his former protégé, now his partner, not his wife, Delma. Last month when he had taken over Owen's role at a business meeting in Singapore he'd found himself unable to contact Owen for a vital forty-eight hours. Their normal practice was to keep one another abreast of all that was happening but on that occasion Owen had simply gone A.W.O.L. But to where?

Lang had seen it as a big shift in the balance of their relationship and it upset him. Over ten years ago, straight from university with an honours degree in commerce and the university gold medal, he had applied for a job with Carter Enterprises, which he quickly secured over a dozen older, highly qualified applicants. He loved the thrill of big business and the high-flying ventures as much as Owen did. He knew he could handle anything Owen threw at him. Which Owen did, the work amounting to quite an overload. But Owen had liked him. Trusted him. They understood one another. Nowadays he had become honorary "family." Owen was allowing Lang to operate at the very top level virtually without input from himself.

There had to be a story. They'd all noticed the big change in Owen but not even Delma had come close to asking what it was all about. If Owen hadn't looked so marvellously fit they might have suspected illness. The only other possible reason for all these mysterious trips away was a love affair, which was quite absurd. In the twelve years Owen had been married to Delma, a very attractive woman some ten years his junior, Owen had never looked sideways at another woman though there were plenty that looked longingly at him. The fact was, and Delma admitted it, she had masterminded a strategy to land Owen. Why not? He was handsome, rich, available. Who was he going to leave all his money to? He needed a wife and heir and Delma had convinced him that she would be perfect.

The marriage had turned out to be durable but not, in Lang's perceptive eyes, what one could call happy. Strictly speaking, it hadn't been a love match. A fact never outwardly acknowledged by either of them but always running on a subterranean current. With a less than ardent husband always preoccupied with business Delma had taken to mild flirtations. Never too overt, Owen for all his calm detachment wasn't the man to cuckold. But recently Owen had become a man of mystery. To track him would have been the greatest insult but Lang found himself frequently pondering exactly what was going on in Owen's life. Owen was a married man with a wife and young son. He was highly regarded in big business and the tropical north where he lived. Why would a man like that want to complicate his life with a secret affair? Providing, of course, the mystery in Owen's life *was* a woman.

Whatever Owen's story, his early life before coming north, he never spoke of it. Otherwise he spoke of anything and everything with his partner. Lang always felt Owen had suffered some terrible blow in his youth. Something he had never dealt with. Owen would probably go to his grave with all his secrets intact.

Now Lang walked at Owen's side totally unaware of the attention his own looks attracted. Lang was and always had been very casual about such things. Achievement was what mattered. He had gone after it traumatized by his father's financial crash, which had literally lost the family farm, though farm hardly described Marella Downs. A ten thousand square kilometre run on the western side of the Great Dividing Range, Marella was a most valuable property. Forsyths had lived there for well over a hundred years, a long time in this great southern land, until his father becoming increasingly desperate after a series of financial busts and industry reversals had finally lost it.

His father had since died, unable to handle not *adversity,* but the burden of guilt he had placed on himself for losing the family heritage. His father had never lived to see him gradually overcome all the terrible setbacks, but his mother had. Barbara Forsyth resided at Marella Downs once more.

He'd made it his life's business to buy back the farm. There was no way now he could run the station. He was too heavily and financially involved with Carter-Forsyth Enterprises. His sister, Georgia, and her husband, Brad Carson, his good friend from childhood, managed the station very efficiently indeed. When it was time, Brad wanted to buy him out. But that was a good while off yet. Meanwhile the Forsyths were back on Marella Downs with the next generation taken care of in the form of one Ryan Forsyth Carson, aged six. His nephew and godson.

Lang and Owen lunched at the club, a beautiful old building that looked out at the Botanical Gardens. Both men re-

laxed over an excellent meal, which was served with quiet
flourish by the waiter who usually attended to them. They
talked easily. It had been their way from day one, but Owen
studiously avoided talking business, which in itself was extraordinary despite the six months of change. Instead he con-
centrated on their outside interests like their mutual obsession
with boats, sailing and big game fishing. They had the glorious waters of the Great Barrier Reef at their doorstep after
all.

A few acquaintances walked in, toting briefcases. Greet-
ings were exchanged. One man crossed the plush ruby carpet
in long strides, patting Owen rather fulsomely on the back.
"How's it going, Owen? You look *good!* Been making some
frequent trips to town, eh?" The snapping gaze was trans-
ferred to Lang. "Hi there, Lang, nice to see you again."

He spoke some more but Lang barely heard him. He was
focusing on something suggestive in the man's manner. To
Lang's sharp eyes it assumed a ribald touch, "nudge, nudge,
wink, wink." That disturbed and angered him on Owen's
behalf.

"What was that all about?" he decided to ask when the
man had gone off to rejoin friends. It had taken time to shake
off his early awe of Owen, but these days he was much too
self-assured, too successful to be intimidated by him.

Owen returned his direct glance unwaveringly. Probably it
would take an earthquake to shake Owen Carter's composure.
"Does it matter? Silly sort of fellow. Anyone would think
I'd turned up with a voluptuous blonde."

"Always supposing a woman would be admitted to these
hallowed halls," Lang returned ironically.

"Actually they can come for dinner." Owen slewed
around to see where the other man had gone. "Wives and
partners of members."

"About time they changed the rules." Lang was of the
strong opinion women shouldn't be excluded from anywhere
they cared to go.

"I'm not averse to that." Owen smiled, signalling their

favourite waiter. He allowed himself a whiskey, rattling the ice cubes against the rim. "Will you see Arthur Knox for me this afternoon, Lang?" he asked, apology in his dark eyes. Apology and something else. Something that would have been in someone else, excitement. "I have things to do."

"No problem." Lang gave him the only answer possible. Arthur Knox was the senior partner of Knox Frazier, and Carter-Forsyth's taxation lawyer. "Will we meet up for dinner?" Both of them were staying at the same hotel.

For once Owen's eyes were veiled. "I'd have liked that, Lang, only I got talked into having dinner with old Drummond. Remember him?"

"Judge Drummond?"

"That's the one."

It was all too pat. In fact it sounded like Owen had rehearsed it.

Out in the street again, the pavement bouncing with heat, they said their farewells. Lang realised it was later than he thought, so he moved off in the direction of Knox's legal offices. Many pretty girls, long legs flashing in short skirts, had passed them as they'd stood outside the club. Owen hadn't turned his head to look at a one of them. So why now was he worrying Owen had somehow got himself heavily involved with a woman? A woman moreover who already had a firm grip on him. This was trouble. No doubt about that. A bloody foolish middle-aged fling? With a marriage to be ripped apart? Young Robbie who was certainly overindulged and overcosseted by his mother nevertheless adored his father. A broken marriage would wreak havoc in the child's life. He, too, would become involved. Even asked to take sides.

Women! One way or other they caused a lot of pain.

Too many people recognised him at the hotel so Lang sought the anonymity of a restaurant rather than the dining room of the hotel, where he usually ate whenever he came to town. The very charming receptionist had recommended a restau-

rant to him and most obligingly made the reservation. He had
toyed with the idea of room service but found the food was
vastly better in the main dining room, which had a well-
deserved reputation for fine cuisine. Besides, he was hungry
after a long day of talking and listening. Talking to their
Malaysian counterparts in a big building venture; listening to
their own legal adviser.

Dressed in a lightweight Italian suit made of the finest
Australian wool he took the lift to the elegantly opulent foyer
then walked out onto the street. The doorman at the ready
asked if he wanted a cab but he felt it ridiculous to take one
over a short distance. He could walk. The receptionist had
given him precise directions. She had also given him a subtle
come-on, which he wasn't about to avail himself of. One
man's indiscretion was more than enough.

The restaurant was new or it had been totally refurbished.
From his walks around the city he didn't remember it at all.
Very obviously up-market. Maybe too much so. He wanted
to be quiet. He had lots to think about. The very smooth
maître d' found him a nice secluded table having ascertained
privacy was what he wanted. The restaurant was not quite
full—Tuesday was an off night—and the tables mainly held
discreet businessmen in well-tailored suits, and their partners,
girlfriends, wives. The restaurant itself was lovely with luxuriant, flattering lighting falling on elegant tables and chairs,
fine china and flatware, gleaming wineglasses. Leafy small
trees in huge copper pots were set at intervals along the floor-
to-ceiling windows that allowed a view of the river and the
city's night-time glitter.

Seated at a window table but lightly screened by one of
the small decorative trees, Lang decided on lobster for an
entrée followed by baby lamb Roman style. He was walking
back to the hotel so he ordered a very dry martini right away
followed by a bottle of fine wine. Not bad at all, he thought,
looking around. A very nice place. Close enough, too, to the
hotel. He wondered how Owen would enjoy his evening.
Gordon Drummond, though very learned in the law, was an

austere man of austere habits. He lacked a sense of humour. Not the most entertaining of dinner companions.

The lobster was superb. Queensland seafood was renowned. The lamb was just as good. He was contemplating dessert, maybe the *terrine di gelato al spezie con pan alle spezie*. Fluent in Italian—tropical North Queensland and the sugar industry owned a great deal to its Italian migrants, he knew that meant a three-spice ice cream with spiced bread and red wine syrup. Like most men, he had a sweet tooth. The waiter was hovering, ready to take his order, only as he looked up he encountered a sight that transfixed him.

Uncertainty became an inescapable reality.

Being ushered to a table was Owen, radiating power, his tanned handsome face glowing with pride. Preceding him was the most beautiful young woman Lang had ever seen and he'd seen plenty of good-looking women. Tallish, very slender, she had masses of silky sable hair, curling loose to her shoulders. The centre part pointed up the perfect oval of her face. Her skin in the soft lighting had the perfection of a white camellia. But the most breath-taking feature was her eyes. From a little distance they looked purple. Surely no one had purple eyes, or were they a very dark blue? Above the eyes arched finely marked brows. Her features were small. It was a style of looks that put him in mind of the young Vivien Leigh of *Gone With the Wind* fame, but for all her beauty and the cool chic of her dress it wasn't admiration he felt. It was condemnation. Pure and simple.

So this was Owen's mystery woman. The catalyst that had released Owen from the traumas of the past. Lang stared at her for endless moments. Without actually looking for Owen's mystery woman, he had found her. She had to be the answer to the great change in his friend. He had never seen naked emotion plain on Owen's face. But he saw it now. Owen had fallen head over heels in love with a woman young enough to be his daughter. The *thought* filled him with dismay. The *sight* turned the fine wine he was drinking to vinegar.

How could Delma contend with this? Delma, herself a striking-looking woman, who worked with what God had given her. He couldn't fail to know Delma had never felt totally secure in her marriage, indeed she trusted him enough to confide in him, though God knows Owen gave her every material thing she and the boy wanted. Everything it seemed except his heart. It was Delma who worked to keep the marriage alive. She was an excellent hostess and a high-ranking committee woman on just about every committee in town. Now everything was threatened just as he feared. He had never seen Owen look so happy, so triumphant, like a man in possession of some grand secret.

Or could it simply be the seven-year itch? An affair that started brilliantly and could only end badly? Owen was a fine-looking man. He had a full head of dark hair, good strong features, a Celtic nose and fine dark eyes. Sadly he had never deeply loved his wife yet love was written all over him now as he moved to a secluded table for two along the glassed wall. Owen was infatuated with this girl. Totally seduced. A blind man would have felt his deep involvement.

Lang exhaled a deep troubled breath. How was he going to get out of here without Owen seeing him? God, he couldn't remember a worse situation. Owen wasn't only his partner, he was his friend and mentor. He couldn't bowl right up and take Owen to task. That would be a massive invasion of Owen's privacy, an invasion Owen, a proud man, wouldn't take too kindly, even from him. All he could do was wait for Owen to confide in him, yet Owen hadn't said a word for the past six months. Obviously he was planning something and he didn't intend telling anyone about it until that plan was finalised.

Seated at their table, Owen had his back to him, broad shoulders square beneath the jacket of his expensive suit. He was free then to observe the way the young woman's eyes were focused on Owen as he spoke. Not once did her gaze wander casually around the dining room as most people's did. It was as though she in her turn was spellbound by him.

help but make comparisons between the girl and Delma. Delma had the style and the particular confidence of a mature woman, but the young face he'd looked into was quite unforgettable.

He slept badly, sure of two things. Owen was never going to release his hold on this girl and two, there was little if anything he could do about it.

He was coming out of the shower when the phone rang. Swiftly he grabbed the hotel's white bathrobe and shouldered into it.

Owen's deep dynamic voice greeted him.

"How's it going, pal?"

"I can't wait to get home." The simple truth.

"Sure you love the place." Owen chuckled, obviously in high good humour. "Listen I know I've been asking far too much of you for quite a while now, but there's a couple of things I need you to do today. I want to take a quick trip to the Gold Coast. A guy there has a motor yacht I want to take a look at. From all accounts it's pretty fine."

"And what's wrong with the *Delma*?" he asked, trying to temper the faint sharpening in his tone.

"Nothing. Nothing. I could put it on the market today and someone would snap it up. This yacht is handmade by Italy's finest craftsmen. Highest quality materials, all the latest equipment. I'd like you to come along as well—we always look at boats together—but this trip we're so pushed for time."

Of course, he thought dismally. Owen intended taking his girlfriend along. Spend the day exploring the delights of the oceanfront. Why the hell couldn't the man speak?

"So what is it you want me to do?" He had little choice but to ask. Owen was the senior partner.

"You could see Rod Burgess for me," Owen said. "You can handle the man better than I can anyway, and maybe pay a courtesy call on the old patriarch, Brierly. He still has a stake in a few of our property developments, as you know.

Again he'll be pleased to see you. One aristocrat to the other. My polish is superficial. Yours isn't.''

"Don't you believe it," he clipped off ironically. "Anyway since when did so-called polish have anything to do with success in business?"

Owen laughed. "I know, I know, but old man Brierly really liked you. Do it for me, pal? I want you to know the best thing I ever did was take you on as a partner."

"And I salute you as my mentor. What time do you expect to be back? Our return flight is booked for 9:00 a.m. Means we have to be at the airport by..."

"Don't fuss, don't fuss," Owen chortled, hugely happy. "By the way, I have some great news for you."

God here it comes. His first reaction was a deep biting anger. Why? When it was all said and done he had no right to interfere in Owen's life.

"It's everything I've been seeking," Owen was saying, his voice thick with emotion. "For all of my life it seems."

"Sounds like it's been making you very happy?" He tried to keep the sadness out of his tone. Who was he to sit in judgment on Owen? Owen had been almost a father figure to him; yet the muscles in his neck tensed as he waited for Owen to continue.

"The answer is a great big *yes!*" Owen's deep voice boomed down the line. "But I'll have to defer the telling. It needs time. Lots of time. I've wanted to tell you for ages, but the timing hasn't been quite right. This has altered my life, Lang. I didn't think it was possible to know such joy. I want to shout about it to the world. I want it proclaimed."

"Can't you tell me some of it now?" he as good as begged.

"I'd love to, mate, I know you're the man to fully understand. I love you like a son, which you're not, thank God. I've got plans for you. I know why people respect you like they do."

"Hey what's all this about?" Owen was throwing out question marks galore.

"Life's too short not to say what we really feel," Owen exclaimed, his emotions uncharacteristically showing. "Listen, pal, there's a knock at the door. I'll go. I've hired a car. See you tonight. We'll have dinner. I want you to meet someone. Righto, righto!" This was obviously directed to the person at the door. "See ya, Lang," Owen spoke briskly into the mouthpiece.

"See you," Lang repeated. "Go with God."

Now why had he said that? It sounded so sombre. Almost final. He sought an answer even as he hung up. Maybe it was a releasing of his own acute tension. Maybe it was because he feared for his friend. A man like Owen, a middle-aged man so much in love, could be badly damaged if things went desperately wrong. He was absolutely certain Owen had suffered emotional trauma in his youth. The poor man could be fooling himself he had found the answer to his life's happiness. There was Delma. There was Robbie. With a divorce a shattered Delma would move away with Robbie. A child needed his father. He should know.

Was it so strange Owen was acting the way he was? Beneath the tightly controlled facade Owen was a passionate man. It was just that he was sorry, so sorry. Sorry for all of them.

Except the girl.

She was kidding herself if she thought snaring a much older married man, a very rich man, was her right. No one could blame her for falling in love but when the outcome was going to cause so much lasting damage it was time to muster real character.

His meeting began with Burgess, a very successful tourism entrepreneur whose operations extended from the Queensland Gold Coast with its glorious beaches and luxury resorts, to their part of the world, the tropical north of the state over a thousand miles away. Rod was delighted to see him, and after a while steered the conversation away from business to talk cricket. Rod was mad about the game and he'd heard he'd been a dab hand with the bat in his university days.

They parted on the most amicable of terms, Rod sending his best regards to Owen. "Tell him from me, his best years are to come!"

A prophecy?

He decided to grab a bit of lunch before seeing Sir George Brierly. Owen had some information he'd like to show the old man in his room. He'd borrow Owen's key from reception as soon as he got back to the hotel. All his nagging worries seemed to be getting the better of him but his working philosophy was to keep going and concentrate on the job ahead. It wasn't like him to feel morbid. A good strong cup of black coffee would clear his head. The coffee Rod served at his office was pretty darn terrible when he thought about it. There was no excuse, either. The coffee plantations of North Queensland were turning out very fine quality coffee, but he'd felt a little hesitant to point that out to Rod who drank his down with every appearance of pleasure. Obviously Rod was a tea drinker.

Reception handed over Owen's key without a murmur. The management knew both of them well. Knew they were close friends and business partners.

In the lift he used the security key to get himself to the top floor. This was the first time Owen had bothered with a suite. Owen, like himself, usually settled for a deluxe room. After all, they spent precious little time in it. His dark thoughts were returning. Was this Owen's little love nest when he came to town? Surely not? Owen wouldn't expose himself or his young love in this way.

He opened the door, seeing the empty space before him; the suite was commodious, comfortable, stylish, a home away from home for the businessman under pressure. He went to the desk along a wall hung with a large genuine oil painting, a seascape, of considerable merit. The hotel liked to trust its up-market guests. He spotted the folder at once. It contained coloured photographs, designs, architectural drawings still in the planning stage for a challenging new project, some twenty-five spacious luxury villas they intended to build along the Hibiscus coast shoreline. The resort would include a private marina, seafront pool and twenty-four-hour security. Last year they'd won platinum in the Best of the New Millennium Awards. He was riffling through the folder when he heard a sound from the master bedroom beyond. He hesitated, frowning. Was it possible the suite was being serviced? With the large folder in his hand he walked to the corridor calling out, "Hello?"

Even as he did it, the warning bells rang. He knew in a very few moments he was going to come face to face with the love of Owen's life.

Hell and damnation. He wasn't ready for it.

She emerged from the bedroom looking disturbed before she even caught sight of him. She'd been dressing. That was clear. She'd probably spent the morning in bed. He took in the silky black masses of waves and curls tumbling to her shoulders, little tendrils still damp from the shower. She wore no shoes on her narrow feet. Up close he saw her eyes were lotus-blue, like her dress. Nor could he stop noticing, like last night, she was trembling. If he were truthful with himself he'd have to admit there was something approaching violence in the emotions that shot through him. He didn't want it, but he couldn't stop it. He despised this girl but he knew now he wanted to see her again. The full realisation shocked him.

"You!"

The word was a little cry, a reminder of the night before. If possible she was more agitated than he was.

"I'm sorry." He knew his voice was curt to cutting. "I didn't realise anyone was here. Lang Forsyth." He introduced himself. "I'm Owen's partner."

"Yes." There was such stillness about her. She might have been a painting. "Owen has told me so much about you."

"How fascinating!" He recognised that as acid. "I must go now." He had to get out of there before he told her what he thought of her. That would be much too much. The end of everything with Owen.

"Please…" It was an appeal and it stopped him briefly. "You were at the restaurant last night."

"I wanted to be private. There's no reason for you to tell Owen. I had no wish to disturb you."

"You looked at me as though you hated me?"

The luminous gaze momentarily disarmed him. "How could I do that? You're a total stranger."

"Except you *do* have a reason. Your reaction was so strong."

He gave a harsh laugh. "What the devil are you doing here in his suite? Half dressed." He marvelled at the colour and texture of her skin.

"I'm a kept woman, is that it?" Such control for such a small-boned, small-breasted, willowy creature.

He knew his eyes were ice-cold. "Forgive me if I can't be as civil as you'd like. All I can think of is what's going to happen from now on?"

"You don't want me in Owen's life?"

He shook his head. "Definitely not."

"But I am in it, Mr. Forsyth," she said with no trace of triumph. "My position has been confirmed. Owen loves me."

"Infatuation," he cut in. "Owen is totally swept away by your beauty."

"He's seen it before."

He couldn't account for that. "What are you talking about? What tricks are you playing?"

"No tricks," she said gently. "If you'd allowed me just a little time to justify my actions…"

He turned decisively to go on his way. "I'm sorry. You'd need all the time in the world."

"You're on dangerous ground, Mr. Forsyth," she warned from behind him.

"Don't you think I don't know that?" He caught hold of the doorknob. "You've propelled yourself into Owen's life but it's not my relationship with Owen that disturbs me the most. Or the fact that our relationship might end. It's Owen himself I'm worried about. Owen and his family."

"Such pure motives. How high-minded you are."

"While you are not." He let her see his contempt.

"I think you'd better go now."

How her flush accentuated the whiteness of her skin. "I intend to. From something Owen said to me earlier I think he was planning for us all to meet over dinner. That may not be possible."

"I'll allow Owen to persuade you," she said quietly. "I have no desire to myself."

CHAPTER TWO

EDEN first laid eyes on her father at her mother's funeral. She had no idea then who he was or the remarkable fact that he, not Redmond Sinclair, was her natural father. Owen was her mother's lover over twenty years before when they were both very young.

Owen—a ruggedly handsome man in his prime—would have stood out anywhere, but it had been the quality of his gaze that had seized and held her attention. Just as Lang Forsyth's silvery lancing glance had compelled her to look in his direction in the restaurant last night. Now she knew who he was. Owen's close friend and partner. Owen had portrayed Lang Forsyth as a wonderful guy. Brilliant! A man of great strengths, educated, polished, ambitious, a great mixer, the sort of man you'd want on your side. Not the man you'd ever need as an enemy, Eden has since concluded.

She put up her hands to cover the flush of helpless anger that rose to her cheeks as she relived that brief incident which had so affected her. Of course he harboured the belief she was Owen's mistress. How ironic! She still saw his frozen gaze. Diamond-hard. Heard the vibrant voice, uncompromising, deliberately stripped of all softness. She comforted herself—just *barely,* he had upset her so much—he would soon know the truth. Not that she would ever forgive him his contempt, understandable or not. She had suffered enough anguish of recent times, but she had loved her mother dearly. It hadn't been easy to accept Owen's claim he had fathered her and not Redmond Sinclair, the man she called "Father." They had never been close or so comfortable for her to call him "Dad." Redmond Sinclair was a man who never showed emotion. Not even at her mother's funeral when every other thing about him spelled grief and desolation.

Now at long last Eden knew what was at the heart of the lack of trust her "father" had shown in her mother. The fear, kept rigidly in control, one day she might leave him. In retrospect she realised Redmond Sinclair had lived with such a burden of suspicion it had poisoned him. It allowed her to understand his reserve with her. In his heart of hearts Redmond Sinclair had known she wasn't his child, but so closely did she resemble her mother, the woman he loved who had never returned his love in full measure, it kept him from rejecting her child outright. That and the fact Redmond Sinclair always strove to please her grandfather who had pulled a lot of strings to further his son-in-law's legal career.

Her grandfather had been shattered by her mother's death. In the intervening six months his health had declined rapidly. It seemed he didn't want to survive the loss of his only child or thought he didn't deserve to. Eden had known since she was a child her parents' marriage hadn't been a happy one just as she had gleaned over the years it had something to do with her mother having obeyed her father's wishes as to her choice of husband.

Eden sank into an armchair trying to recover from the great shock of Lang Forsyth's dramatic entry into her life. The day had started out so well. She had stayed in town with her father rather than return to the "family" home where she no longer felt needed or wanted. These days she only presented a pain-filled reminder to Redmond Sinclair. Her real father, Owen, had turned over the master bedroom of his suite to her while he spent the night on the very comfortable day bed in the main room. He'd left early to inspect a motor yacht he was particularly interested in. It was moored at the Gold Coast, some fifty miles away. She intended to spend the day in town doing some shopping and having lunch with a girl-friend. Owen would be back late afternoon. He had every-thing planned. At dinner he was going to introduce her to his close friend and partner, Lang Forsyth, a man Owen clearly looked on as "family."

How the best-laid plans came unstuck. Lang Forsyth had caught up with her many hours before Owen intended, his attitude harshly judgmental. In truth the sight of him at dinner last night, a stranger staring so fixedly at her, darkly handsome and authoritative, an easy elegance to his tall body, his beautiful clothes, had filled her with foreboding. His appearance in Owen's suite this morning was as momentous in its way as her first meeting with her own father. Even when Forsyth found out who she really was, Eden had the feeling he would always be antagonistic towards her. Maybe that was her destiny. Always to be the outsider.

Eden sank further into her reverie. She and Owen had come a long way since their first meeting. After her mother's sudden violent end in a car crash, she and Redmond Sinclair had been on compassionate leave from her grandfather's legal firm, Redmond a full partner, she a recent associate. Owen had approached her one morning as she'd left the house to visit her grandfather. At first she'd been startled to see him again, thinking perhaps he was someone from the press—there had been some speculation her mother's death hadn't been an accident, but Owen by his sheer presence overcame any fears and suspicions. He told her he wanted to speak to her about her mother; Cassandra was someone he had known very well when they were young. Could they go someplace quiet and private where they could talk?

Strangely she had gone with him without a moment's hesitation, his demeanour so gentle and protective it allayed all fear. They had coffee but it was actually when they were seated on a park bench looking at small children playing on the swings that Owen began to relive the past....

"My story, the central tragedy of my life is no means unique, Eden," he told this beautiful young woman gravely. "It's a story as old as time. Star-crossed lovers. Boy from the wrong side of the tracks meets and falls desperately in love with the adored only child of a rich man. You know your grandfather. He was, and I suppose remains, a man who had very exacting standards. Penniless young men of no family had no place in his scheme of things. Despite that, for long tumultuous months Cassandra and I were lovers. But in the end the pressure from your grandfather was all too much for Cassandra. She'd been reared like a princess. She couldn't contend with a run-away marriage to me. I had absolutely nothing to offer her at that time. Save my love.''

''It wasn't enough?'' Eden asked, the tears shimmering in her eyes.

''Your mother did love me, Eden. I want you to know that. But your grandfather and security won out.''

''How sad. My mother was always sad.'' Eden stared sightlessly at the playing children. There was more. She just knew it.

''As was I.'' Owen sighed deeply. ''It has been an unparalleled grief to me all these long years to know my beautiful Cassandra was carrying a baby when she married her store dummy.''

Eden was electrified. ''My God, what are you saying?'' It came out like a plea. For a long moment she couldn't speak until Owen put his arm around her shoulders.

''I'm saying, my dearest girl, that baby was you. Had I known your mother was pregnant to me at the time, things would have been very different.''

''You mean she didn't tell you?'' Eden shook her head, shocked and aghast.

''Not for three long years into her marriage. I have a letter to show you. You will know her handwriting. It confirms what I'm saying. The letter was sent to my mother who died without even knowing she had a granddaughter. Cassandra couldn't trace me. I was mad with grief after she married. I felt crushed by her betrayal. I packed up and left home. I went north of Capricorn to frontier country. My mother always regarded Cassandra with some trepidation. She foresaw what would happen.''

"Yet she sent you the letter?"

Owen's voice was gentle. "She had great integrity. I never told her about you because I knew she wouldn't have left things alone. She was the wise one. Your mother begged me in the letter to keep her secret just like the confessional. Though it opened the door to unimaginable pain, I did it. Cassandra could always manipulate me. She convinced me you were happy and secure. So was she. As some kind of sop, probably to diffuse the inflammatory nature of her revelation, she told me she had named you after my mother, of all people. Your grandmother, Eden Carter."

Eden was silent, trying to absorb her shock. "This is unbelievable," she managed finally. "I can't take it in."

"I understand. I understand all about pain, suffering and shock. Read the letter." Owen withdrew the yellowed much-read, much-folded pages from his inside breast pocket. He passed it to Eden….

As she read it her eyes became so filled with tears she had to pass it to Owen to finish aloud. How had her mother ever done him such a terrible wrong? Had she no courage? Whatever had persuaded her to remain with Redmond Sinclair? The marriage, so badly foundered, had never been happy but as a highly "social" couple they had maintained a public fiction. She herself had missed out on a father's love. She could feel it pouring out of this man she now knew to be her real father. Redmond Sinclair had tried hard to find a place in his heart for her but he never could get the portals open. Such love as he had, more like obsession, had been reserved for her mother.

It was a terrible story and they all had paid for it. Even her grandfather had been worn down, she now realised, by a sense of guilt. In persuading his daughter to marry "one of their own kind" he had committed her to a life of unhappiness and unfulfillment. A charade.

"You know there's been some speculation my mother's death wasn't an accident?"

Eden turned her head to look directly into her real father's fine dark eyes.

Owen looked off abruptly. "Cassandra would never have left you."

"You didn't know her all these long years. I expect my mother changed greatly from the girl you knew. She was a sad woman. But so gentle and beautiful, everyone loved her. The man I called Father all my life certainly did."

Owen's rugged features hardened to granite. "I'm sorry, Eden. I don't want to hear about him. Sinclair was the one Cassandra chose over me. From the look of him he hasn't weathered the years well. He used to have a shock of golden hair. He was very handsome, very eligible, a promising lawyer. I never got past grade ten. I had to leave school before I was sixteen to learn a trade. There was little money in our house to go around. Today's a different story. I'm a very rich man."

"Did you ever marry?" Eden asked, thinking of so many broken lives.

Owen nodded. "I have a wife and child. A little boy called Robbie. Robert after my father. My wife, Delma—she has Italian blood—calls him Roberto."

"Then you're happy." She was glad.

"I should be happy." Owen frowned. "I *would* have been happy if I hadn't had you and Cassandra perpetually on my mind. Often when I'm alone in my boat I have the habit of calling your name. Eden! My little girl. Sounds desolate, doesn't it? It used to frighten the gulls away. But now by the grace of God I've found you. Cassandra's tragedy has set us free."

They'd met regularly after that, a couple of times a month. Owen travelled from his home in far North Queensland to be with her. Such was the power of blood both found their relationship, though propelled forward at a great rate, an intensely accepting one. They talked easily and freely, both of them on the same wave length. In fact Eden had come to

recognise she had inherited some of her father's character-
istics, even mannerisms, though she had grown up isolated
from him. There was so much for them both to discover.
They enjoyed hours and hours of discussions and confidences
as they pieced together the past. Owen was determined she
come to live with him, to be family. But Owen in his exultation at finding a lost daughter was running the risk of al-
ienating his wife and the mother of his son, her half brother,
Robbie. It was obvious in keeping his friend and partner,
Lang Forsyth, in the dark he had done some considerable
damage already. But Owen couldn't be persuaded to speak
out prematurely any more than she could. Both of them
needed time to turn their lives around.

While her relationship with Owen blossomed, her troubled
relationship with the man she had called "Father" for all of
her life deteriorated to the point Eden felt Redmond Sinclair
no longer had anything to say to her. It was time to move
out. Not hastily. People were talking enough already about
her mother's untimely death. She had no wish to cause
Redmond extra pain and embarrassment. Six months after her
mother's passing it mightn't seem such a desertion.

She hadn't confided in her grandfather. Had she any need
to? Her grandfather doted on her almost as much as he had
doted on her mother, but he had become so much frailer Eden
held back from upsetting him in any way. He surely knew
the truth. She was convinced he did. Her grandfather was a
very clever, astute man. He and her mother had been so close;
her mother would have poured out the whole sorry story.
Then there was the time factor, though no doubt she had been
passed off as premature. The depth of her grandfather's
grief—he was inconsolable—began to persuade Eden he had
profound regrets at the way his daughter's relatively short
life had turned out.

Eden rose from the armchair and returned to the bedroom
where she finished dressing. She was looking forward to
lunching with her friend, Carly. They had gone to school and
university together. Like her, Carly had taken a degree in

Law and joined a firm specialising in Family Law. Carly
would have to get back to work, but Eden had taken accu-
mulated leave from her grandfather's firm not only to max-
imize the amount of time she could spend with Owen, but to
spare Redmond Sinclair the painful memories the sight of her
must evoke. Cassandra had been the one to hold them together. Now that she had gone, so had the bond. Proof pos-
itive if she ever needed it she and Redmond Sinclair were
not of the same blood.

After a companionable lunch with her friend, Eden did a little
leisurely shopping then returned to the hotel late afternoon.
Owen should be back from the coast by now. No doubt the
new owner of a luxury motor yacht. Later in the evening
they were to dine with Lang Forsyth. A dinner at which
Owen proposed to reveal her true identity. That should put
the arrogant judgmental Lang Forsyth very nicely in his
place. Strangely enough she gained no pleasure from the
thought. Owen thought the world of him.

Lang Forsyth looked what he was, a man from a privileged
world who nevertheless knew what it was like to fight to
survive. Physically he was very striking. Well over six feet,
very lean but powerfully built; she had noted the wide shoulders. A highly individual face; dark, very definite features,
arrogant high-bridged nose, the mouth quite sensuous, hol-
lows under the high cheekbones. The whole impression was
one of tremendous vigour and vitality, the excitement coming
from the ice-grey eyes. A total surprise when his hair was
near black and his polished skin was tanned to dark gold.
She was sure that Lang Forsyth would never be her friend.
Not in a lifetime. But he was Owen's close friend and partner. She had to remember that.

The sound of the phone in the quiet suite surprised her.
She picked it up, murmuring, "The Gold Suite."

"Miss Sinclair?"

She drew a sharp breath, already aware of the caller's identity. "Yes, Mr. Forsyth."

"I'm in the lobby," he said, his tone almost flat. "I'm coming up."

Suddenly the air-conditioned room seemed cold. Unease entered Eden's mind. What was it he wanted? This wasn't the time for confrontation.

She went to the door at his knock, opening it and standing back. His striking face was drained of all expression though she thought there was a pallor beneath his tan.

"Sit down." He spoke more gently than she had yet heard.

"What is it?" She was so used now to unhappiness and grief she instantly caught his mood. "Is it Owen?"

His dark brows contracted. "I don't know a *good* way to tell you this. Owen has been involved in a three-car pile-up on the Pacific Highway. It seems the driver of one of the cars suffered a seizure of some kind, ploughed into the first car, while Owen's ploughed into him."

Her knees went from under her and her eyelids flickered. "Oh My God!"

The next thing she knew she was lying back in an armchair with Lang Forsyth tapping her wrists. "Are you okay?"

"I knew something was wrong." She kept her head down, unaware he was standing over her with an expression of concern, not unmixed with worry about the difficulties she now presented. Delma had to be informed. Owen had been conscious for a good part of his ordeal, giving the police his name and particulars and the person to be contacted.

Owen, as in so many other things, had left it to Lang to break the news. To Owen's wife. And his mistress. He hadn't rung Delma yet. Indeed he was with this girl, even trying to protect her.

"Where is he?" she raised her dark head to ask; her violet gaze resting on him.

He named the hospital, hearing her heartfelt sigh. "I'm sorry. I should have told you it wasn't fatal."

"My mother's was." She spoke very quietly.

He steeled himself not to react. "I beg your pardon?"

"My mother was killed in her car just over six months ago," she told him from the depths of her grief.

"I'm very sorry." Her news appalled him. "That must have been a great grief and a great shock to you. *Now this.* I'm going to the hospital now." He could no longer delay.

"I'll come with you." She rose from the chair, trying very hard to calm herself.

"I don't think that's a good idea." He couldn't hold off his frown.

"I don't care what you think," she said, without challenge. "If you don't take me I'll get a cab. I want to find out exactly how Owen is. I love him. I'm not going to lose him now."

Her intensity was such he believed her, yet he had to chide her. "You must remember he has a wife and child."

She looked at him as if that had no significance. "What has that got to do with me?"

Oddly he felt no anger. Just a quiet despair. "You don't look callous." In fact she looked the most sensitive of creatures, her beautiful eyes glistening with unshed tears.

"Owen had intended to tell you all about me tonight," she said, as though she pitied him.

That restored his hostility. "Frankly, Miss Sinclair, that fills me with dismay. You must realise this is going to be a very difficult time. I have to contact Delma, Owen's wife."

"I know."

There was a secrecy to her, to Owen, he couldn't fathom. "Why haven't you done it before?" she asked. "Why not before telling me?"

Why indeed. "I don't have to explain myself to you," he answered with more force than he intended. "We both know I have concerns about you. You'll have to get out of this suite. I'll attend to everything."

"Of course." She inclined her dark head. "I'm so grateful you're here with your odd combination of condemnation and concern. Are you going to take me to the hospital?"

Her insistence left him reeling. "If I can trust you to keep perfectly quiet. I feel sure Owen's accident is going to be reported. There could be news people about. Owen is quite a celebrity. Most certainly in the North.''

"And I'm someone second rate?'' she asked with gentle irony, fixing him with her soulful eyes.

He couldn't bear to think of her and Owen together. "You're a young woman who's happened to make a bad mistake. I can't claim to understand Owen's motives in not telling me about you long before this. We've shared so much over the years I've worked with him.''

"He thinks very highly of you,'' she said. "My identity will come out soon enough. If not while Owen is ill then sometime in the future. Should anything happen to him, God forbid, I'll quietly disappear.''

He found he didn't want this to happen, yet he spoke curtly, cursing himself, but driven by shock and anxiety. "You may think that *now.*''

"What are you so afraid of? Do you think I'm after Owen's money?''

"Forgive me if I believe Owen's money is a factor.''

She shook her dark head. "You couldn't be more wrong. My mother left me financially secure. There's my grandfather, also. You know nothing about me, Mr. Forsyth.''

"Except you've got my friend, Owen, spellbound. Anyway, what good's talk? If you're coming with me, come. If you've got belongings here, get them. I assume if you're so financially secure you have a good home?''

She flushed, the sheen of tears in her beautiful eyes. "You're making far too many assumptions as it is, Mr. Forsyth. If you give me a moment I'll pack what I have. We were to have had dinner with you tonight, instead Fate has stepped in yet again.''

They never spoke a word throughout the fifteen-minute journey to the hospital though Lang found himself watching her continually in case she started to crumble. He even had to stop himself reaching for her hand. Such a slim wrist, a network of delicate blue veins beating there. Two gold bracelets.

He knew gold. Both were unmistakably heavy eighteen carat. Patek Philippe watch with diamonds and a mother-of-pearl face. All very expensive items. Had Owen given them to her? He rarely gave Delma presents though he allowed her to buy whatever she liked. For *herself.* There was a huge difference. He was beginning to feel more and more sorry for Delma. She would take it very badly when she found out about this girl. He was silent under the great surge of anxiety he felt. What if Owen died? God, hadn't his own father slipped so easily out of life?

"Are you ready for this?" he asked as they made their way to the ward.

Her voice rang with hope and conviction. "I know he's alive. I'm sure of it. He won't leave me. Not now."

"You look like you're going to faint." Indeed she was snow-white. Her took her arm as stabs of pity pierced him, his manner at that moment more protective than he realised. She was tall for a woman but beside him she seemed so *small.*

"I haven't fainted so far, have I?" Her lips moved.

"You did briefly at the hotel," he reminded her. "Anyway, we're here now. Please let me do the talking."

"Of course." She didn't look at him, but she didn't pull away, either. That had some significance but he didn't want to look into it now. This was Owen's young love.

The surgeon was waiting for them, and they briefly shook hands. He needed to scrub up. "Mr. Carter will undergo immediate surgery," he told them, looking from one to the other as though they were a pair. "For internal injuries. He's bleeding and has broken ribs and a broken collarbone, but he's in good shape for his age. He's conscious at the moment, but he's been sedated. You can speak to him for just a moment, if you like. Now you must excuse me."

Even as the surgeon turned away they saw Owen being wheeled out into the corridor.

"Come on," he heard himself saying to her, upset beyond words at the whole damn business.

Owen's dazed eyes rested on him first. "Lang!" He put up a hand and Lang took it, feeling the strange chill off Owen's skin. "We're here for you, Owen," he said, allowing his strong feelings to show. "Eden is here, too." He used her name knowing that he liked it. It suited her.

"Eden?" Owen tried to turn his head, clearly excited, agitated and the medical attendant shook a warning head at them.

She came forward, taking Owen's other hand, bending over him, her lovely face as sweet and innocent as a Madonna's.

The expression that blazed out of Owen's face caused him to look away. This was love. *Real* love. God! And it was going to last. He knew that now. No one, not wife, not child, not partner, was going to separate them.

Ward Sister came up briskly. "Thank you," she said with what was clearly a dismissal. "Mr. Carter is due in surgery. You're waiting?"

"Yes." He spoke for both of them. "We want to be here."

Sister nodded. "There's no telling how long it might be."

"We'll wait." Eden spoke for the first time. "We couldn't possibly leave."

But Owen wanted desperately to detain them. "Lang," he called, his voice weak and slurred.

"Go now," Sister said. "You're disturbing the patient."

"I think he wants to tell me something." Lang started to move back towards Owen but Sister stepped with authority between them.

"If you don't mind." She lifted a hand to signal a medical attendant who wheeled Owen away.

He sat Eden in the waiting room, a cup of coffee in hand before he put through a call to Owen's home from the privacy of the empty corridor. He had spoken to the Carter housekeeper initially, not filling her in before he had a chance to speak to Delma, but he had left the message for Delma to ring him on his mobile the moment she got in. The housekeeper sensing something was wrong had apologised profusely for not knowing exactly where Mrs. Carter had gone. Mrs. Carter was a busy lady, sometimes she forgot to say.

It seemed an age before Delma's call came through. He saw the girl's eyes as he left the waiting room again. She seemed to know intuitively this was Owen's wife.

Delma didn't take the news calmly. She was a volatile woman, her cries so despairing they echoed quite stridently over the phone line. It was as though Owen couldn't possibly pull through. He tried his very best to reassure her but in the end had to fall back on telling her he would ring the instant they had news.

"That was upsetting?" The girl's eyes flew to his as he took a chair beside her. They were alone. Another couple had been there, but they had left.

He nodded, not surprised by her perceptiveness. "That was Delma. She's quite distraught."

"She loves him," the girl said as though that explained it. As indeed it did.

"I couldn't convince her she will see him again." He thrust an agitated hand through his hair.

"It must be terrible to be so far away."

That incited his retort. "Would you have risked being here had Delma been in the city?"

She looked undismayed. "Of course. But then Owen would have made things clear."

"That's childish talk," he answered, and shook his head. "You truly believe Delma, his wife, would just walk away? Miss Sinclair, you don't know her. I wouldn't care to see Delma humbled and humiliated. She wouldn't react with quiet dignity. She'd turn into a tigress before your eyes. I don't think that's an exaggeration. Certainly for her son, Owen's heir."

"Tell me about him," she invited, speaking in a gentle tranced tone. Perhaps she was in shock. "Robbie. Roberto?" She longed to say "my little brother, my half brother," but she had given her word to Owen he would be the one to break their grand news.

"My godson," he said with deliberate irony. "I have another. My sister, Georgia's, boy, Ryan. Both boys are of an age. Why do you want to know?" He allowed his eyes to move over her face, feature by feature, almost dividing it up into segments like a painter. Above and beyond the physical perfection of her features was a quality that gave her real power. Sensitivity? Mystery? Refinement? Maybe it was all three.

"I want to know everything about Owen," she said. "He's told me so much but you have a different perspective. Certainly of me."

"Can you blame me?" he asked with heavy emphasis. "Owen has a wife yet he's obsessed with you."

"Obsessions aren't uncommon."

"Especially with women like *you*."

Tension fairly crackled in the air around them. "Why don't you tell me what you *think* I'm like?" she invited, not avoiding his lancing gaze, but suddenly challenging it.

"I have no desire to make you unhappier than you are." He kept his voice toneless. "You realise Delma will be flying down to Brisbane?"

"I'm surprised she's not already on a plane."

"Then don't be surprised at all the complications. I assume you're not going quietly?"

What else could she say? "Owen wants me here," she answered gravely, almost certain Owen, facing surgery and unsure of the outcome for all the surgeon's reassurances, had been about to divulge their "secret" when Sister intervened.

The surgeon in his operating greens, made an appearance much sooner than either of them had anticipated. His expression, as was the case with so many doctors dealing with life and death on a day-to-day basis, was austere.

"Oh God!" Eden gave a soft moan, every muscle in her body contracting. She wanted to believe everything was all right, but she was still traumatized by the death of her mother. She would never get over those shock moments when Redmond Sinclair, bone-white, had come to her office to give her the catastrophic news the police had found the wreck of her mother's car. Cassandra was dead. Now Eden breathed in and out fighting off dread.

"It's too early, isn't it?" She appealed to this hard, strong, commanding man, Lang Forsyth, but he, too, looked like he was preparing himself for bad news. "What's it been?"

"An hour ten." A V-shaped cleft formed itself between his definite brows.

They were both on their feet, both persuaded the relatively short duration of the operation might mean the worst.

"He must go on living. He *must*. He can't die." Eden didn't realise she was muttering aloud. Finding her father had given her own life meaning. She couldn't lose him now. Her distress communicated itself to Lang at an intense level. He found himself putting a supportive arm around her, encircling her slender body. At the same time he felt a deep thrust of desire within him which he didn't much welcome. It was dangerous, even shameful. The odd part was she leaned into him for all the world like she trusted him utterly. It was as if they were *friends*. But then she was desperate for comfort and support from anywhere. Even from *him*.

Only when the surgeon reached them did he give a brief but illuminating smile. He shook hands first with Lang, then Eden. "I'm happy to tell you everything went well." He eyed them almost cheerfully. "Mr. Carter is a remarkably fit man. His heart is strong. We've repaired the internal injuries, stopped the bleeding. Orthopaedics will be looking at the collarbone. As you saw, he has some fairly extensive facial and chest abrasions, but they will heal. He's been taken to the recovery room. You can see him for a few moments when he regains consciousness."

The relief was enormous. Eden could feel the swoosh of blood through her veins. "I've got so much time to make up.'' She spoke with deep gratitude. ''So has Owen. Now our whole world can expand.''

He looked at her with disbelief. Keeping his tone level was a physical effort. ''I wonder if you'll say the same a year from now?'' he asked soberly. ''I'm not sure I could be happy walking over other people to achieve it. I know it happens all the time but these are my *friends*.''

His tone though quiet all but savaged her. Eden felt if she couldn't speak out soon she'd become unstuck. Thank God, Owen would be able to make things abundantly clear very soon. She wanted to wipe away Lang Forsyth's deep concerns. She wanted to be free of that daunting stare. She wanted to come out with the truth.

I'm Owen's long-lost daughter. Just like in a work of fiction. I'm the daughter he never laid eyes on until six months ago. Only she knew Owen was set on revealing the whole story to his friend, rather than her.

Once more, Eden watched Lang Forsyth walk away to make his phone call to Owen's wife. She'd thought many times over the past months Owen could have told his *wife* of her existence. The fact he hadn't made her wonder anew about the state of their marriage. If the marriage was strong, she had a chance of being accepted. If the marriage was rocky Owen's wife wouldn't want any reminders of her husband's past love right under her nose. In his exultation at finding her Owen appeared to have given little, if any, thought to the repercussions on his marriage. And what of young Robbie, his father's heir? He mightn't want a ready-made grown-up sister. One, moreover, to whom his father found no difficulties with demonstrating his love. Eden knew intuitively many problems lay ahead. All of them were merely human with human faults.

Eventually they were allowed to go to Recovery where they found Owen conscious despite his facial lacerations, looking better than they'd thought, but as expected, very groggy.

"How's it going?" Lang bent over his friend, showing his relief and affection.

"Fine, pal." Owen tried hard to sound normal but even for Owen the feat was beyond him. "Thanks for everything, Lang. I owe you so much. Where's my beautiful girl?"

"Here, Owen." Eden went forward, as she did so, the expression on Owen's face almost embarrassing in its exclusion of the rest of the world.

Eden looked like she desperately wanted to hug him. She was half crying, her eyes for Owen alone.

"Don't cry, sweetheart," Owen was imploring, his voice hurting but boundlessly tender.

Lang found once more he had to turn away. This was all too damned disturbing. It was going to alter lives. He knew, too, when he was beaten. Delma, God help her, had yet to find out.

In a little space of time they were ushered out. Owen was in no condition for more than a few words, though by sheer force of will he brought up his arm to wave at them as they moved through the door.

In the corridor Lang turned to look down at her. Tears were sliding silently down her face, yet she looked radiant. It was fascinating to see and it was driving him crazy.

He still had the use of the hire-car. It was parked in the leafy street, a short stroll from the hospital entrance.

"Your overnight bag is in the car," he reminded her as they walked down the driveway. "I have time to drive you home." Some knight, he thought. She was evoking such strange contradictory emotions in him; he had to fall back on simple good manners.

"I can get a cab," she offered, giving him just a glimpse of a smile so sweet it touched the heart he had hardened against her.

"I can save you the trouble. Just tell me where you live?"

"Really you don't have to."

He cut her short. "You've had a shock. Owen is my friend. He would want me to look after you."

"But *you* don't have to?"

The thing was, he *did*, but he denied it almost sharply. "I guess I don't." He took her arm quickly to cross the busy road. "Well, maybe not altogether. You're so young."

"You can't be all that much older?" She picked up the conversation when they were in the car, the strange intimacy reforming.

He gave her a tight smile. "A thousand years. I'm sure of it. I'm nearly thirty-two as it happens and you're...?"

"Twenty-four. I can't believe my mother would have gone and left me just before my birthday."

"It was a car accident, you said?"

She didn't answer; simply nodded her head. She knew she would choke up if she began to explain. Her grief over her mother's death, so recent, would never subside. She was frightened, too, to begin thinking in terms of guilt. Had it really been suicide? Was she in some way to blame? She thought she had always been there for her mother yet her mother had never confided the true circumstances of her birth. That hurt her. Or hadn't her mother been brave enough to say? Her true parentage had been a closely guarded secret until the very end.

That fact alone presented Eden with an enormous emotional hurdle.

They said nothing more to one another until they were on the freeway.

"You must know the city well," she ventured, deeply regretting her own lack of truth. He hadn't asked how to get to her suburb.

"Yes I do," he clipped off.

"Owen's wife must be tremendously relieved," she continued gently. "Is she flying down?"

"Of course."

He wasn't inclined to talk, his handsome profile remote. Eden glanced out the window. It was dusk and the glorious tropical sunset was turning the city's glassed towers and high-rises to glittering gold. In another ten minutes night would fall, as it did in the tropics, suddenly and completely, as if someone had thrown a switch. The multi-coloured sky, now rose, gold, scarlet, indigo, lime green at the horizon, would turn to a deep velvety purple. There were people everywhere. The picturesque paddle wheeler, the *Kookaburra Queen* was returning from a river cruise; the City Kats busy ferrying passengers across the river to the parks where they kept their cars.

She loved her home city. It had a delightful, leisurely way of life and a wonderful climate. Owen wanted her to go to live with him in North Queensland. To think of the number of times she had visited the Great Barrier Reef and the magnificent Daintree Rain Forest and had never known her birth father, Owen, was close by. She could even have driven past his home. There were some wonderful tropical homes in the far North. Fabulous sites overlooking the spectacular beauty of turquoise sea and emerald offshore islands.

"It's been an extraordinary day."

"Yes."

"Are you only going to answer me in as few words as possible?"

He responded wearily. "Eden, what is it you want me to say?"

"You can say I accept you?"

His brief laugh was grim. "The only way I could accept you is as Owen's long-lost child."

Her heart shook. "How do you know I'm not?"

Another lancing glance. "I know Owen, that's why. There's no way in this world Owen would have deserted his child, his child's mother. I *know* him. No way he could have kept such a thing secret. Not from me, let alone Delma."

"You don't think she would take kindly to having Owen's love child fostered on her?" she asked, her voice so poignant he wanted to stop the car to confront her.

"You're not pregnant, are you?" God, he didn't think he could live with that.

"I find that unforgivable." She had never done anything illicit in her life. Owen was her *father,* for God's sake. What code had Owen bound her to she couldn't say it? Both her mother and her father were good at keeping secrets she'd found. She wasn't going to relive history. Tomorrow when Owen was a little stronger she was going to insist he explain the exact nature of their relationship and the whole sad story behind it. There was no earthly reason to delay, not even Delma's arrival. She was tired of this charade and intensely angry with Lang Forsyth. She didn't enjoy how he was making her feel.

"I don't follow you at all," he was saying. "In fact we seem to be speaking a different language. This isn't a good situation. You must know that. I feel I have to warn you, you'll have a job fending Delma off. She's a tough mature woman. She'll fight tooth and nail for her man." God knows she had come up with quite a strategy to land Owen in the first place, he thought. But he wasn't about to tell the girl that. It could only amount to extra ammunition.

CHAPTER THREE

ANTAGONISM seemed to cling to them. Antagonism and a strange intimacy he tried to hold down. He wanted to be out of the car. Away from her. The scent of her. She was quite unreachable.

Sometime later he drove into her leafy street. He could see now what she meant when she said she was financially secure. The street was lined with wonderful old Queenslanders, the traditional nineteenth-century timber houses built especially for the tropics, with their wide, deep verandas shading the exterior walls and pristine white wrought-iron balustrades and detailing. The style of architecture could be seen all over the giant state of Queensland extending to his part of the world, the far North where there were fine examples. All these homes were proudly owned and maintained wherever they were, so eagerly were they sought after.

As he glanced out he could see colonial white wooden palings that linked the fences visually with the houses behind it. Masses and masses of pink, white and red oleanders ornamented the fence; towering palms defining the long drives. The street and house lights provided so much illumination he could see splashes of brilliant colour from all the tropical plants in the gardens. Gorgeous scarlets, vivid yellows, vibrant pinks.

"It's the next one on the left," she said quietly, breaking the silence. She pointed not to one of the beautiful big Queenslanders with their large gardens, swimming pools and tennis courts, but to a great two-story Victorian pile, set well back from the street, hiding behind high stone walls and hedges of what looked like sasanqua camellias.

It was an unexpected house for such a girl. He felt she

belonged in something not so overtly ostentatious. Something very gracious. More like the houses that fanned out to either side.

"Your family live here?" he asked, peering out. It was a huge house by any standards. She could scarcely rattle around in it by herself.

"My...f-f-father." Surprisingly she stumbled over it when usually her speech was as clear as cut glass.

"And what does your father think about what's happening in your life? Or doesn't he know...?" he couldn't prevent himself from asking.

She half turned, held out her hand. "Thank you so much, Mr. Forsyth, for bringing me home."

She had the air of a princess in her lovely blue silk dress.

He took the slender hand she extended, little currents of electricity cutting into his nerves and running up his wrist. He had a sudden powerful urge to go inside. Meet the father. He wanted to discover what all this was about. He wanted her, or her father, to reveal something about themselves. He was forced to think of the next day. Delma would be arriving. He was meeting her at the airport. Taking her first to the hotel and then straight on to the hospital. The image of the two women meeting flashed across his mind. He thought of Owen's eyes, his face, his voice and the transparency of his emotions. Everything about him gave away his love for this girl.

Not caring what she made of it, he moved swiftly out of the car, going around to the passenger side.

"I'll see you to your door," he said, helping her out, his manner decisive.

She shook her head. In fact she seemed to him suddenly perturbed. "You don't have to do that."

He stared at the beautiful face pearlescent beneath the street lamp. "I'm assuming this *is* your home." It was just possible she was trying to trick him.

"Not for much longer." Her voice quivered with emotion.

"My God, Eden, do you want to ruin your life?" he exploded, feeling some despair. This could only end badly.

She startled him by touching his hand. "I swear to you Owen will explain everything tomorrow."

"Owen can't make a wrong right," he told her bleakly.

"You just don't *know*," she said, watching him lift his strong elegant hands in a genuinely forced resignation.

"I'll escort you to your front door nevertheless." His frustration was bordering on anger. "There don't appear to be too many lights on?"

"My f-f-father will be home."

There it was again, the tiny stumble. My God, what sort of a father was he? Anxiety prickled his skin.

Inside the extensive grounds he reached out and grasped her arm. She put him in mind of a filly about to bolt. In what direction he didn't yet know.

"Please, you can go back," she insisted.

"What the devil is worrying you?" He stared down at her in the dark. He couldn't grasp what was going on here.

"It would be much simpler. This is a very unhappy house since my mother died."

Six months ago. About the same time she met Owen. Something sparked in his mind then disappeared.

The porch light came on and a moment more he heard the sound of a man's voice. "Is that you, Eden?"

"Yes, it's me. I have a friend with me." She turned to him very quickly in the scented darkness, the flowers immobile with no breeze to stir them. "Oh please, back me up. You're a friend. You've brought me home."

"And I suppose you were staying with yet another friend?" he asked with weary irony. "Okay. You don't seem to be talking much to your father."

"It's not like that," she said.

A tall, rather gaunt man was standing in the open Gothic doorway, the light from the hall chandelier glittering over his metallic-grey hair.

"Well, my goodness, you've decided to come home?" he said. The voice was cultured but infinitely detached.

Eden mounted the short flight of stone steps. "I'd like you to meet a friend of mine," she said. "He was coming this way so he gave me a lift home."

Lang revealed himself very quickly, at a loss with the father's attitude. "Mr. Sinclair?" He moved further into the light. "How do you do? Lang Forsyth."

Whatever Redmond Sinclair was about to say turned to something else when he saw Forsyth step into the light. Tall, commanding, handsome, and many other things beside.

One of us, thought Redmond Sinclair, a snob to the boot-straps, and breathed a sigh of relief. Someone who might very well take care of Cassandra's daughter. "Good evening, Mr. Forsyth." Sinclair used his smooth legal voice, putting out a hand. "It was kind of you to bring Eden home. I was starting to worry about her. Are you coming in?" He wanted to see more of this young man.

"Thank you, no," Lang declined. "I've many things to attend to."

"You're from Sydney?" Sinclair couldn't hide his curiosity. He would surely have met this striking young man had he lived and worked in the city.

Lang shook his dark head. "North Queensland. I'm only in the city for a short time."

"Could I come to the hospital with you tomorrow?" Eden suddenly intervened.

"Hospital, what hospital?" Redmond Sinclair turned to her.

"A mutual friend was involved in a car accident this afternoon," Lang explained.

"Oh? Which friend, Eden?"

"I'm sorry you don't know him, Father. Will you do that for me, Lang?" she appealed to him across her father's gaunt frame.

What could he say? He didn't much like Sinclair. In fact he didn't want to leave her in that house. For a father and

daughter they seemed quite separate. No wonder this girl had
looked elsewhere for love. Found it in a father figure. It happened. He nodded, treading carefully. "It's a private hospital,
Eden, so we can go anytime. Say I pick you up at ten?"

"That's fine," she answered, a shade breathlessly. "I'll be
ready."

She'd be in and out before Delma arrived, he decided.

Eden was moving rather nervously up the staircase when
Redmond Sinclair detained her.

"You come and go as you please, Eden," he observed
quietly.

"I'm sorry." Eden turned around, shocked by how much
weight he had lost. "I didn't think you cared all that much.
But I didn't want you to worry."

"Your grandfather didn't know where you were, either."
Sinclair moved a weary hand across his brow.

"I haven't spoken to Grandad for a couple of days. I've
been in town. I met with my friend Carly for lunch, did a
little shopping. I'm trying to cope with my grief just as you
are."

"And it's only the beginning," he groaned. "I fell hope-
lessly in love with your mother when I was just a boy. There
was never anyone else. Everyone knew we would marry. I
felt I had *everything* on the day I married her, but it was
never enough for your mother. We were never happy."

"I'm so sorry," Eden answered without evident sincerity.
"I know how much you loved her."

"Ah yes, but she never loved me. She met up with someone when she was just a teenager, you know. Some rough
character from the wrong side of the tracks. *He* stole her
heart."

"I'm sorry." Eden was aware she was repeating it like a
dummy.

"Yes, you're sorry." Sinclair sat down in a hall chair,
shaken. "You're a good girl, Eden. I don't think you've one

ounce of deceit in you. I couldn't say the same of your mother. She thought killing herself would set her free.''

''But she didn't kill herself,'' Eden interjected passionately. ''It was an accident.''

''I'd give anything to believe that,'' Redmond Sinclair said so simply, pangs of pity stabbed her.

''Please don't torture yourself,'' she begged. ''She left us both.''

''And I know why. Do you think I haven't noticed you don't call me 'Father' anymore?''

Eden felt like the breath had been knocked out of her. She felt she had no choice but to say, ''Our whole life has altered. I'll always honour you as the man who reared me.''

''Thank you. You're not mine, are you?''

Eden sank down onto the stairs. ''Cassandra lied to us both.'' She could think of no other answer.

''I always knew,'' he sighed. ''I spent a lifetime pretending to be a gullible fool. I'd have done anything to keep Cassandra. To keep your grandfather's favour. It was all *his* fault. He knew from the beginning.''

''You should have all faced the truth. The truth might have set us free.''

''Alas it was not to be. I want you to know I'm fond of you, Eden. You were such a beautiful little girl. I would have adored for you to be my child. Cassandra's deceit spoiled our whole relationship. Still, for what it's worth, I admire and respect you. I'm proud of your achievements. You're a clever young woman. I hope you get the life you deserve. As for me, it's too late.''

Eden dismissed that with a sweep of her hand. ''It isn't at all,'' she said with some spirit. ''You're a man in his prime.''

He shook his head. ''I was young and handsome once. Unhappiness has aged me terribly. Anyway, Eden, I'm going away. I don't know where yet but I'm a rich man. I'll travel. There's no earthly point in staying here. Your grandfather doesn't want to lay eyes on me anymore. He's feeling the guilt. The house is yours. Your grandfather damn near bought it anyway and Cassandra never liked it.''

"I don't want the house, Redmond," Eden said quickly. "It has too many unhappy memories for us both. Perhaps we can put it on the market?''

He ran a hand over his gunmetal hair. "I already know a number of people who would buy it tomorrow. Do it up. I'll organise for you to have the money. I want to do this for you, so don't shake your head. I've done precious little else. And this young man, Forsyth?'' His voice picked up. "He seems rather splendid. Old money, by the look of him. What does he do?''

Eden was grateful she knew a lot from Owen. "Lots of things. Property, investments, rural. He owns the family cattle station. It's run by his sister and her husband. His great interest is horses. He and a partner acquired a thoroughbred stud a few years back.''

"Good grief! He sounds like a paragon. I hope he's not married?'' He lifted worried eyes.

"No, he's not.'' Eden tried to smile.

"Well he's very protective of you,'' Redmond Sinclair, the astute lawyer, stated, thoroughly startling her. "Just stay with him, my dear, if you can. There's a man who will never let you down.''

Eden woke early, grateful that by the end of today the long charade would be over. She had rung the hospital last night before she went to bed, now she rang again asking after Owen's condition. She was put through to his ward, where she was asked if she would like to speak to Owen herself.

Of course the answer was yes.

Owen sounded much brighter, more like his old self. "Some part of yesterday, before the crash, I had the terrible fear I might lose you,'' he confessed, "that's before the paramedics arrived. They tell me I'm doing well. I'll be out of here in no time.''

"I hope so,'' she said. "Lang is calling for me at ten.''

"I know. His call beat yours by about a minute."

"You have to tell him, Owen." She sounded as serious as she could.

"There's no reason why you can't call me *Dad*," he responded.

"You *have* to tell him, Dad." She was thrilled to use that wonderful word.

"Of course I'll tell him," Owen's voice rang down the phone. "I'll tell the world."

"Tell Delma first," she advised.

"I will, sweetheart. Don't fuss."

"I'm just a bit worried." She knew instinctively Delma would feel hurt and very vulnerable.

"Everything will work out fine," Owen told her in his self-assured way. "What do you think of Lang?"

"What does he think of *me* more like it?" She saw her little grimace reflected in the mirror. "With all this secrecy he's got hold of the idea I'm your girlfriend."

"Good God!" Owen sounded genuinely amazed. "Couldn't he see the paternal look in my eyes?"

"Apparently not," she told him wryly. "I'll be enormously pleased to have you set him straight."

"I will, my darling, I promise," Owen chuckled, speaking as though outraged feelings could be healed in a moment.

She was waiting outside the front gate when Lang arrived. Right on time.

"Good morning." He was out of the car, vividly handsome, his glance moving in such a mesmerizing way over her.

"Good morning." She hoped she wasn't flushing, but that was the consequences of seeing him again. "I've spoken to Owen."

"So have I."

"Yes he told me." Now that the play-acting would soon be over she felt calmer.

"I knew he would. He sounded a lot better."

"Yes, isn't that wonderful?" She slipped into the passenger seat while he held the door.

She was very conscious she had spent some little time selecting her wardrobe for the day. Casual but chic, her outfit comprised a cool camisole top, matched with a full skirt with a lovely floral print. The violet colour of the top picked up exactly the pansies on the skirt, as did the sandals on her feet. She knew she would probably be facing Delma, Owen's wife, but it wasn't Delma she had dressed for.

He got in beside her, fixed his seat belt, started the engine. "How are you?"

"I'm fine."

He pulled out smoothly onto the road, shaded both sides by feathery jacarandas that in a few weeks would burst into flower.

"Forgive me if I'm over-stepping the mark, but you and your father don't appear to have come together in your grief?"

The truth is he *isn't* my father. She longed to come right out with it, but she had given her word to Owen. "We've never been close," she said.

"How very sad." He shook his head a little. "I loved my father. My family was devastated when we lost him."

"Then you know all about grief?"

"It's rarely absent from life. But I made my grief work for me and my family. My father through a number of unfortunate investments was forced to sell our family home. An historic cattle station in our part of the world. I bought it back."

Of course he would. She didn't doubt it. "You must have worked very hard?" Owen had spoken of the depth of his commitment, his brilliant entrepreneurial flair.

"I did nothing *but* work," he confirmed. "I had a limited social life. Owen kept me hard at it. He introduced me to people. I in turn was able to introduce him to the Who's Who in the rural world. My family's world. I discovered, too, I had a money-making talent, which mercifully continues to this day.''

"So you'd be quite a catch.'' It was the first she had spoken anywhere near playfully.

"I haven't thought about it,'' he answered, without a smile.

"But you must have given thought to continuance of the Forsyth dynasty?''

"What do you think?'' he said, giving her a quick sidelong glance.

Some shimmer in his beautiful sparkling eyes rocked her. She realised he was astonishingly sexy. Up until now she hadn't wanted to admit it.

"Have you a special lady friend?'' She couldn't believe she said that. It just came out.

"Why the interest?'' His tone was sardonic.

"It's possible we'll see a lot of each other.''

It was at once pain and pleasure. "That's your heart telling you that. Your intelligence might tell you something quite different. You realise I have to go to the airport to pick up Delma. You'll need to be gone by the time we get back. It would never do for Owen to have to face a terrible scene. Believe me Delma is quite capable of making one.''

"With her husband in a hospital bed?'' Eden couldn't help asking.

"I'm very much afraid that won't stop her. Woman-like she'll realise at once you're the cause of Owen's mystery trips. He's been making them for the past six months without explanation to anyone.''

"That was wrong. He's made it hard for both of us but he's a man who must have his way. He'll explain *everything* today. He's given me his solemn promise.''

His eyes were lit with something like pity. "Well when Delma goes up in flames just remember what I've said.''

Owen was sitting up in bed in his private room, the lacerations on his face perversely looked far worse than yesterday.

His left arm was in a sling for his broken collarbone, his wound hidden beneath his loose pyjama jacket, but he managed to flash a big smile the instant they appeared at his door.

Eden went to him, arms outstretched, cupping his face between her hands. "Hi…Dad." She bent to whisper meaningfully into his ear.

"Good morning, my darling," he responded, his deep voice full of emotion. "Great to see you, Lang." He put out a hand to his partner. "You've never seen me have a single sick day since we met."

"I'm hoping you won't have any more." Lang went forward to grip his friend's hand. "You gave us some bad moments," he told him wryly.

Owen nodded. "I had a few bad moments myself. But thank the good Lord my number wasn't up. Sit down. Please…sit." He gestured to the chairs, speaking a shade excitedly.

Lang brought up two chairs, saw Eden seated at the bedside, remained standing by the window removed from them. "I don't have a lot of time, Owen," he explained. "Delma's flight will be in at eleven. I'm picking her up at the airport. She's very anxious to see you."

Amazingly Owen nodded happily. "And my boy, Robbie?"

"He's not much good on a long flight as we know. Delma left him at home with the housekeeper. She'll take him to school, bring him home, look after him." Lang hesitated, then looked directly at his friend, marvelling at his attitude. "Forgive me, Owen, but I think I ought to ask what Delma will be walking into. For that matter what I'll be walking into. I've left it to you to tell me, but your accident seems to have precipitated a crisis. I want to make it plain I'm thinking of you, of Delma, of Robbie, of Eden even. It would be cruel for Delma to have to confront her."

Eden gave a little broken laugh. It had occurred to her many times that Delma, when she discovered her husband had kept so much from her, would turn on her as the scape-goat.

"Tell him, Owen," she urged, dismayed Owen needed so much prompting. "You can't possibly keep silent."

Owen touched her hand, his dark eyes full of old griefs. "I've kept silent so long dredging up the past is a truly terrifying thing." He shifted his gaze to his partner, who continued to stand motionless by the window. "Since I've known you, Lang, I haven't kept much from you," Owen began. "We've been closer than friends and partners. We're darn near family."

Here it comes, Lang thought trying to shrug off the hard constriction around his rib cage. He didn't think he could face this. The upshot would be chaos.

But Owen was still talking. "Twenty years ago I discovered I had a daughter," he said. "The woman I loved, the woman who bore her was Cassandra, Eden's mother."

"What?" Shock ripped through Lang combined with an anger approaching rage. "God Almighty, Owen," he burst out, "how is it possible you didn't tell anyone? Forget *me*. But what about Delma, your wife?"

Owen looked like every word had hit home. "I went to speak a million times but I lost heart. Or the guts. Take your pick. In a way I self-destructed."

As did my mother, Eden thought reaching over and clasping her father's hand. "You've found the courage now." Even as she spoke Lang Forsyth's condemnation bore down on her.

"Cassandra and I were both young and passionately in love." Owen tried hard to explain how it was, but nothing could recapture their grand passion. "I was penniless in those days. Her father was totally against me. In the end he won. He and the man Cassandra married. She was carrying my child."

"And you let it happen?" Lang's brilliant eyes flashed. What went on in Owen's head he now considered beyond him. Did anyone truly know another?

"I didn't know until much later." Owen tried to defend himself, from the intensity of his expression reliving the past. "It was three years into Cassandra's marriage. She wrote to me. Try to understand, Lang." He looked at his friend's dark shuttered face. "I know we're different on lots of levels. I know you wouldn't have reacted as I did. But Cassandra begged me to keep her secret. She told me she and our child were happy and secure. She had named her Eden after my own mother."

"Good God!" Lang shook his raven head almost dumbly; thinking this woman Cassandra must have spent her life living a lie. It seemed extraordinary to him anyone could act that way. Cassandra and Owen. As for Eden! She'd made a complete fool of him by allowing him to believe she and Owen were sharing an intense affair. Couldn't she have spoken out? Except she chose not to. He glanced at her, his expression grim.

Her beautiful eyes were deeply troubled as well they should be. "You're shocked aren't you?"

"I'm not only shocked, I'm totally at a loss. I can't understand how either of you could have allowed me to believe your relationship was other than it is."

"But I never for a moment considered you thought any such thing," Owen protested, totally unaware Lang had seen them together. "Good God, man I may be many things, but I don't take up with bits of girls. I'm a married man. Eden is my daughter. She's part of me. My own flesh and blood." Now Owen sounded outraged.

"Well you've taken a long time to discover it," Lang bit off, not caring in that moment if he and Owen went their separate ways.

"I had my reasons, Lang," Owen said quietly, reading his partner's expression.

"I'm sure." Lang looked through the window, sunlight streaming over his tall striking figure. "Who am I to judge you anyway?"

"You're my good friend," Owen said. "Hold tight to that.

I don't expect you to understand. I truly don't understand myself. Sometimes I think my capacity for loving went with Cassandra. You didn't know her. She was truly unforgettable. She's haunted me for more than twenty years. I attended her funeral. It was there I first saw my daughter. In the midst of tragedy I tell you I knew *elation!* It was *my* time with my daughter.''

Lang turned back to face the man in the bed. ''And it's been Eden you've been meeting all these months?'' Now the pieces were falling into place.

Owen nodded. ''It hasn't been easy for Eden. She's had to come to terms with her short history. She's very loyal to the memory of her mother but she's had a lot of pain and hurt feelings to confront. We needed time to work things through. I had every intention of telling you at dinner. I tried to say something before they wheeled me away to the theatre. But it was not to be.''

''Try to understand.'' Eden turned fully to appeal to Lang. ''Deceit was never intended. It was just an unfortunate charade. Dad wanted to tell you the whole story himself.''

''But surely his accident presented a dilemma?'' His silver eyes slashed over her, hard and challenging. ''Anyway the truth is out now. It might not sound like it—I think I need a little time—but I'm very glad for you both. Finally Owen might know some peace.'' Lang shot his blue linen cuff and glanced at his watch. ''I'll have to go now if I'm to meet Delma's plane. Needless to say I won't be telling her any of this.''

''*I* won't be here, if that's what's worrying you.'' Eden stood up, an enchanting figure in her very pretty clothes. ''Dad must tell Delma alone.''

''I'd prefer if it you were here,'' Owen said with curious insensitivity.

''Listen, Dad. I *can't* be.'' A bright warmth enclosed her. She didn't know if it was anger or not. Anger with herself. With Lang Forsyth, his high mettled head thrown back, staring down his nose at her. Or anger at her father. Owen had allowed the past to dominate his life. Worse, he wasn't being fair to his wife. Eden knew who was going to get the blame for that.

"All right, sweetheart, whatever you say," Owen relented. "I just thought if Delma saw you she would understand everything."

Eden was amazed. Didn't her father know women at all? "Understand what, Dad? That I'm the image of my mother? The girl you loved. I don't think I could risk it."

"Maybe you'd like to come with me," Lang offered, in a clipped voice. "I can drop you off at your home before continuing on to the airport. You have no car."

"That's a good idea," Owen broke in, perhaps with a certain falsity. He really wanted Eden to stay but although he had forced her to keep her peace regarding their "secret" he could see she was determined on going her own way now.

"That was a brief visit," Eden remarked when they were back in the car.

He pulled out into the traffic, unspeaking.

"At least it will give Dad time to get his story straight," she continued.

His voice was deeply ironic. "How much time does he need? He's had twenty years."

"You're very unforgiving aren't you?" Eden said, looking straight ahead.

"Compared to some, I'm a hero. The patron saint of family. I don't much like being made a fool of either, Miss *Carter*. I dare say that poor devil Sinclair didn't much like it, either. I wondered what was wrong between you two."

Eden thought about that, moved on. "I didn't know he wasn't my father until Owen approached me and showed me my mother's letter."

"And then it all fell into place?" He spoke with deliberate black humour.

"I didn't have a happy childhood if that's what you mean. But the man I called 'Father' for all of my life tried to do his best by me. I had everything I wanted. Education, clothes, travel.''

''No doubt your grandfather would have had something to say about that if you hadn't. He seems to figure very largely in all this.''

''My grandfather is a broken man.'' Eden spoke quietly, his upset with her and Owen obvious.

''Your mother left a trail of broken hearts.''

Undeniable. ''So she did, but I think she was just a catalyst for other people's emotions.''

''A bit of a problem. Don't let it happen to you.''

She inhaled deeply. ''I'm a lot tougher than my mother. A lot better educated. She didn't get to finish her studies. I have a law degree.''

''Then you should know all about frauds?'' He glanced at her, his eyes scathing.

''I *wanted* to tell you. Did you think I liked the way you looked at me?''

''You expect me to believe Owen bound you to silence?'' he challenged her. ''I thought silence didn't exist for women.''

''That's a cheap shot.'' Her violet eyes darkened. ''It was his story after all. You'd have been told when the time was right. It was sheer chance that made you dine at the same restaurant we did. I didn't know who you were then, either, but I was shocked by the way you were looking at me. The disdain. You do it terribly well.''

''Do please accept my profound apologies.'' He gave a brief laugh. ''Owen or no Owen, I would have put it straight.''

''I dare say.'' He was a decisive man of action yet she couldn't fight the taunt. ''You seem like a very trenchant person.''

''Trenchancy has its uses. And Sinclair. What does he make of all this?''

''Why should I tell you?''

Another glance. "Oh, for goodness' sake, weren't you the one who said we were going to see a lot of each other."

"I think I'll have to brace myself for that. My adoptive father only admitted last night he'd always known in his heart I wasn't his child."

"So you can't stay there." He frowned as if she were in some sort of danger.

"Where? You mean my own home?"

"That's exactly what I mean," he answered curtly. "People can turn ugly. Surely you know that? Sinclair is a man betrayed. He must have his moments when he knows blind rage."

"More like terrible coldness. He would never harm me," Eden said. "Redmond Sinclair is a man of the law. He's going away very soon. He intends to travel. He wants me to have the house or the proceeds from its sale. It could already be sold for all I know. Many people appear to want it. It may be a mausoleum but the right architect could alter the facade."

"So you're an heiress?" Another brilliant glance.

"I told you I'm very comfortably placed."

"How nice. Owen, however, figures in the Rich 200."

Eden stared out at the broad deep river carrying its ferries. "As do you."

"You've checked?"

"Hardly. So you can spare me the sarcasm. Owen told me making money is your thing."

"Owen is worth a great deal more."

"That means nothing to me." She thought for a second of asking him to stop the car but she'd had her comeuppance.

"That's good," he clipped off, "because Delma sees her son as Owen's heir."

She studied his handsome profile, the strong elegant hands on the wheel. He was a very confident and expert driver. "How much money does one person need?" she asked quietly. "Money has never made my family happy. I know lots of people who live full contented lives without wealth."

"It's handy to have it all the same," was his sardonic reply.

"I still say it's not essential." Eden bent her head, her voice low and full of apology. "I want to tell you how sorry I am that I had to deceive you. Would you please forgive me?"

It was a very poignant appeal delivered by a very beautiful, repentant, young woman, but he reacted as if the very air would ignite.

"Sorry, Miss *Carter*. It's too late."

CHAPTER FOUR

FEELING like some inexorable process had been set in motion, Lang waited a good hour before he returned to the hospital. Owen and Delma had much to talk about he thought grimly. He had no wish to be around. Although Delma had his sympathy—Owen really didn't pay her anywhere near enough attention—he was well aware Delma had set up any number of domestic arguments. No doubt due to her insecurity. Though she was far removed from being a woman scorned, Delma's big problem was that Owen had never loved her as a man should love his wife. In essence, Owen had devoted his emotional life to a *memory*.

He knew he was having a bad attack of disillusion with Owen, his mentor. The whole thing was beyond him. What sort of people were Owen and his Cassandra? Both of them had treated their daughter only in terms of themselves. Every child has a right to know who their birth parents were. Everyone needed their emotional roots nourished. It hadn't happened for Eden. If he weren't so damned—what? He couldn't really express his truly contradictory and confusing feelings.

If she hadn't made such a fool of him, he could find it in his heart to forgive her deception. But the strange hostility wouldn't ease. It was like a constriction around his ribs, yet it carried its own excitement. He thought for a moment. Unwarranted guilt?

His physical desire for her had manifested itself the moment he laid eyes on her. It made him feel raw and vulnerable. He didn't much like sensations which resulted in so much upheaval. He'd had enough of that in his life. The emotional jangle could well be compounded by his loss of

esteem for Owen. By the same token, he had never thought
himself so judgmental. If anyone had asked him to account
for his actions of late he'd have been at a loss. And that was
another cause for concern. Nowadays he liked to think of
himself as a man in control. God knows it had taken so much
mental stress to work the family's way out of perilous circumstances and re-instate his mother's life-style. Perhaps
he'd have to put his feelings for this girl down to some kind
of fear of another crisis in his life? On the one hand he'd
wanted to *protect* her; but when she had appealed for his
understanding he had cruelly rejected her. It was so unlike
him. He was a man at war and that was a highly unstable
way to be.

When he'd dropped her off at her home—even more of a
monstrosity in broad daylight—she had thanked him with
quiet courtesy. He knew she had fire in her, he'd seen the
flashes in her beautiful blue-violet eyes, but her whole manner was governed by a gentle discipline that was probably
due in part to the circumstances of her life and heightened
by her legal training.

It wasn't the end of the dilemma, either. Owen was a married man. He had to appease a wife who was already on
emotional short rations. Owen would be hoping to see his
newfound daughter every day. Eden had given every indi-
cation she wanted to see her father. Now there was Delma
to head up the triangle. A very great deal depended on how
Delma would react when Owen told his grand secret. Very
clearly it served to explain the less than happy state of their
marriage.

From the moment he walked into the room it couldn't have
been more obvious the private talk had gone badly. Delma
looked a wreck. He wanted to turn and leave—let them face
it together—but couldn't. Owen was in no state to handle
combat. He was signalling with his eyes he needed support.
The whole business was getting messier and messier. Delma
would probably never accept Owen's daughter. He couldn't

imagine, either, Owen would allow Delma to over-ride his decisions, or interfere with his plans. He was even beginning to believe Owen wouldn't think twice about ending his marriage if he thought Delma was going to do something so incredibly foolish as to say she wanted Eden banned from the house. Knowing Delma as he did Lang wouldn't have been all that surprised.

As he stood at the door, Delma looked up, all the muscles in her long tanned neck tense. "Well he's finally spilt the beans," she said, pointing accusingly to Owen. "Not a word about his past has passed his lips for as long as we've been together, now *bucket loads!*"

Owen grimaced. "Delma the drama queen! I've told her we'll manage. It's not as though I've been unfaithful to her. Eden is beautiful, isn't she, Lang?"

"Beautiful, clever, enchanting." There was no point in mentioning she was far more than all three. Delma appeared desperately hurt and angry. Trying to allot blame. And why not? Frankly feeling the way *he* did, he couldn't blame Delma for feeling betrayed.

"You didn't know anything, Lang?" Delma appealed to him, as her long-time friend and confidant, a role, in fact, pushed on him.

"Don't be a fool, woman," Owen interjected sharply. "You know enough about Lang to realise he would have urged me to confide in you."

"So why didn't you?" Delma demanded, looking almost haggard in her distress.

"Frankly, my dear, I don't think it was your business," Owen responded far too bluntly. "All this happened a long time ago. Long before I met you. I doubt if I would have done anything only Cassandra died."

"Cassandra!" Delma lashed out. "What sort of a woman was she? You say it all happened a long time ago? Apparently it's not finished yet. It mightn't ever be finished. It could go on and on. What does she want, this girl?"

Lang answered as Owen turned his head to the window.

"She wants her father, Delma. Plain and simple. Looking back at her life she realises the man who had that role offered little in the way of love. I've met him. He's another one who allowed himself to be trapped in the past. Whatever love he had in him, he gave to Eden's mother."

"I just don't believe this!" Delma, a woman lacking that particular sort of magnetism, rubbed her temple. "Isn't this Cassandra supposed to be dead?"

"Very dead." Owen spoke harshly, fine dark eyes blazing. "My love affair with Cassandra was over twenty-five years ago. I regret not having spoken to you of the central tragedy of my life, Delma. It would have explained so much about me."

"It would have explained why you don't love me." Delma's eyes were fixed intensely on her husband.

Owen attempted a shrug, winced in pain. "You knew what I was like when you took me on, Del. You wanted me right or wrong as they say. I've tried to do my best. I've never been unfaithful to you."

But Delma's expression was tense and bereft. "This feels like death," she said painfully. "The death of a marriage. I won't walk away from it with nothing, either. And I'll have custody of my son."

Owen gave an ironic bark. "So much for a woman's compassion. Cassandra gave me none. Now you. While you're working out your strategies you might consider what's your real problem? Eden is no threat to you or Robbie. She's a warm, compassionate creature. What are you, Del?"

"I want to see her, Lang," Delma said determinedly when they were back in the car.

"That's up to Eden, Delma," he said quietly. "She has to answer to no one. I should tell you she's no push-over. She might have lacked a lot of love in her life, but she hasn't lacked material things. She's had an excellent education. She's a lawyer, working in her grandfather's firm. Quite a prestigious one as I've since found out."

Delma had little interest in that. "What does she look like?

Is she like the mother? *That's* what bothers me.'' Her voice, one of her most attractive features, was flat with jealousy.

"I wish I could tell you she doesn't resemble her mother, Delma, but Owen admitted she's her mother all over again.''

"I suppose we can thank God she is his *daughter* otherwise he might have fallen madly in love with her all over again.''

Lang glanced at her with open censure, his eyes cool. "I don't think it helps to talk like that, Delma, even in your anger and hurt. Owen may not have done the right thing as far as we're concerned, but knowing him as we do, it's obvious he's suffered through the years. Eden is his *daughter*. He lost her and mourned her for all these long years. Now they've been brought together by Cassandra's death.''

"How did she die?'' Delma asked abruptly.

"In a car crash.'' He said nothing about the speculation attached to that.

"There's so much mystery surrounding that woman,'' Delma said. "Was her father more important to her than the man she loved?''

His father's opinion had been very important to him. Lang remembered that very clearly. "Owen was little more than a boy,'' he tried to explain. "He worked as an apprentice to a boat builder. Hence his knowledge about and interest in boats of all kinds. Cassandra was an only child. She couldn't live with her father's disapproval.''

"You mean she couldn't live in a less than privileged situation. Gutless, I call it.'' Delma's voice cracked.

"It doesn't matter now,'' he sighed. "Cassandra's life is over. For all she complicated her own and other people's existence enormously.''

"I knew Owen had secrets,'' Delma lamented. "But no way did I think of this. Please do something for me, Lang. Ring her. Use your car phone. Just tell her I want to say hello. It won't take long. I'll stay in the car, but it's crucial I see her.''

* * *

Eden answered the phone on the third ring. She recognised his voice immediately and understandably there was a moment's hesitation as he put Delma's request to her.

"I take it she's very upset?" she asked quietly.

"Yes." That went without saying, but what an understatement! "Just a brief meeting. Delma is tired and she has no wish to disturb you. She'll remain in the car. Perhaps you could come out to us."

"No problem," she answered, sounding very much like she could handle it. "I'll be on the lookout for the car."

"Ten minutes," he said.

The massive wrought-iron gates hung wide open when they arrived. Electronically controlled they'd been shut earlier in the day so he surmised Eden must have activated the switch to open them.

"So we're not dealing with a little farm girl," Delma observed, looking up towards the very large, very pricey piece of real estate.

"We're not *dealing* with Eden at all," he pointed out with another obscure flash of anger.

Delma's response was dismay when she first caught sight of the girl. Eden was moving swiftly, gracefully along the circular driveway, the breeze lifting her long hair and fluttering the hem of her pretty dress. "What wouldn't I give to look like that!" Delma spoke defeatedly.

He tried to brace her. "You're a very attractive woman yourself, Delma. Don't hold it against Eden because she happens to be beautiful."

"Ah, yes, the genetic factor," Delma grimaced. "My poor Owen. He didn't have a chance."

He brought the hired BMW to a slow halt. Eden, unsmiling, but looking serene, came alongside. "Lang," she acknowledged him with a soft, sideways glance, her attention directed towards the woman in the car. "Hello there!" Now she smiled, her whole demeanour warm and friendly. "I'm so very pleased to meet you, *Delma*. May I?"

Delma tried desperately to keep her emotions under control, but in the end couldn't. "You and your father have been meeting for months," she burst out, high colour in her face. "Why now?"

Oh no! Lang thought wearily, thinking everything was turning into a shambles. Delma had promised she would remain civil.

"Six months isn't a long time, Mrs. Carter," Eden was saying "I'd call twenty-four years a long time. I had no word from Owen in that time. I'm so very sorry you're upset. I can see that you are. I want you to know I understand how you feel."

"How could you?" Delma laughed dubiously, beyond hearing the sincerity in the younger woman's voice.

Clearly it wasn't the time to talk so Eden stepped back from the car. "Perhaps we can speak when you're less shocked?"

"Oh goodness, yes!" Delma gave a cracked laugh, hating herself, hating this girl with her beautiful face and her fine composure.

Lang stepped out of the car, determined to cut the meeting short. "I'm sorry," he apologised to Eden, leading her away. "I should have known better. I haven't made so many mistakes in years." Another great difficulty he had to contend with.

"You're by no means the only one." She turned back towards Delma. "Goodbye, Mrs. Carter," she called. "Please believe it when I say I'm no threat to you. Or to Robbie."

"You mean *my son!*" Delma thrust her head out of the car window aggressively.

"And my half brother." A flame in Eden's violet eyes sparked. "At least he's had his father for all of his young life." With that, she turned swiftly on her heel.

Lang found himself going after her, catching her without effort although she was moving like a gazelle. "It's her pain and frustration talking. *Please,* Eden." He tried to appeal to her. "Hurt has afflicted us all."

"Yes it has." She swallowed down a rush of shame and humiliation, staring up into his taut handsome face. Something powerful drew her to him, those brilliant light eyes on her setting off a tremulous shock. She realized, but for the deception that lay between them, the betrayal, they would undoubtedly have been drawn together. "Mrs. Carter's reaction is understandable," she said, "perhaps even reasonable given so much has been kept from her. But that woman will never like me. I know that for certain."

He could well have agreed, instead he said, "Give her a chance. When she's less stressed."

"It has nothing to do with stress." Eden continued walking back to the house. "She will never forget the part my mother played in Owen's life. She probably never knew what was going on in her married life, now the knowledge will engulf her. For very obvious reasons she won't want me around. I'll only serve to remind Owen of my mother."

"That's awkward, I know." By now they had moved into the shelter of the Gothic doorway. Just for a moment he lost control of his hand. It caught the point of her shoulder—he could feel the delicate bones as he turned her to face him. "Your mother tragically is dead. You'll have your own life to lead. You'll marry. Have a home of your own. Owen isn't going to dominate your life."

"No he isn't." She shook her head so forcefully her loose dark mane was set in motion. "No man is ever going to dominate me. I can take care of myself. I've been doing it for most of my life."

He tried to be as patient as he could and he wasn't by nature a patient man. "I'll take Delma back to the hotel. See her settled. I'm not family, you know, though God knows I always seem to get involved." Delma was too much in the habit of using him as backup, but he didn't tell Eden that. Instead he said, "Owen is at fault here whichever way you look at it." He couldn't possibly add "and your mother," that would have been too cruel. "I've had countless business hassles to confront over the years but I don't think I've ever felt as frazzled as I'm feeling now. Have lunch with me. I didn't have much breakfast and I'm hungry. How about you?"

"Are you suggesting we start again?" Her soft voice held the merest silky taunt.

"We can try." He met her direct gaze with one equally intense.

"Dad must have been terribly upset if Delma feels this way?"

He made a sound of exasperation. "Owen is as tough as tempered steel. I'm afraid if he hadn't had an accident and been hospitalised I'd have said he had it coming."

"So you've distributed the blame fairly. Part Dad. Part me."

It was too true. He glanced back over his shoulder to the car where a no doubt seething Delma was waiting. "Eden, I don't have time to argue or analyse," he said, trying not to sound curt but not succeeding. "I don't even have the inclination. Delma is waiting. I'll drive her back to her hotel. Owen is in good hands. Let's just have lunch. I can be back in about thirty minutes."

"Fine." Eden responded with cool calm, when her mind was racing. In many ways this man was her enemy. And he was such a mixture! So tough and hard, yet it was equally true he was trying to find common ground. She could have declined his invitation, but she hadn't. He was far too compelling and he had touched off a deep sense of challenge.

Under an hour later they were sitting at a corner table at an excellent out-of-the-city restaurant with a fresh contemporary look. The perfect place to relax but both of them were decidedly edgy, as though by being together they were taking a risk.

"What about sea food?" he asked, flooded by a kind of delight in her presence, lapped over by a profound wariness that had something to do with the power of her beauty and feminine allure.

"It's very good here." She nodded, glancing around at the other couples at the tables. Most were young, arty and deep in conversation, faces full of vitality and sexual invitation.

"Then the lobster?" He glanced up from the menu, seeing the shadows in her beautiful, violet eyes. She looked entirely without artifice but she couldn't be free of it, he thought cynically.

"Why not."

She said it elegantly with a little wave of her hand, almost as if it didn't matter what he ordered, she would like it.

"A glass of wine?"

"Just one. Perhaps a chardonnay. This has been a hard time for me."

"I don't mind telling you it's been a hard time for us all," he said with a trace of black humour. "Owen's actions over many long months have been quite inexplicable and therefore upsetting." He lifted a hand to signal the waiter who responded immediately, threading his way through the tables.

"Well it shows." She reached over and tentatively touched his hand. "Please let me say again I'm sorry for the deception."

"I just wish you'd have been more open." He wanted to take her slender fingers, but was careful not to.

"It was what I wanted." Her skin tingled from contact with his. Her heart pumped harder.

"Only Owen didn't judge it the right time?" His voice mocked her.

"Maybe he isn't as perfect as you are," she retorted very quickly, trying to shift the weight off her heart. The waiter arrived and she sat back, a little shocked at herself, allowing him to order for both of them. She had never had a penchant for saying dangerous things before but this man brought out a hidden recklessness.

The white wine when it arrived was chilled and beautiful, full of fruit flavours and refreshing acids.

"What are you thinking?" he asked, watching the way her mouth rounded lusciously as it touched the wineglass. Hers was a mouth just begging to be kissed.

"Oh, wouldn't it be wonderful if we could miraculously wash our world clean."

He shrugged. "The past always stays with us," he said. "One thing is certain, all of our lives will change. Owen will want to keep you by him. Once found, you won't get away."

"I can tell you're very disillusioned with Dad?"

He knew he appeared to be coolly scrutinizing her but in reality he was soaking up that beauty and femininity like a sponge. "Owen has been very good to me." He leaned towards her. "I can never forget that. He's been a true friend. It's just that he chose to keep so much that was absolutely vital about him from us. We're not talking the grand love affair of his youth here. The consequence was you. His daughter. Small wonder Delma is shocked."

"And that bothers you?" she asked. "What exactly is Delma to you?" It was an awful thing to say but she said it, wanting to challenge him as he was challenging her. "Is it possible there's to your friendship than meets the eye?"

His silver eyes very nearly smoked. "Oh, don't be absurd."

"It's obvious you really feel for her." She stared into his handsome, arrogant face.

"I've known her since forever," he clipped off. "She's a friend. I've seen the best and worst of her."

"Is it possible you once had an affair?"

The beautifully cut mouth showed both disdain and amusement. "Now you've added something entirely new to the script."

"If it's any consolation I know that." Eden dipped her head in apology. "But you are close."

"Because I'm Owen's friend and partner and Robbie is my godson," he answered with faint heat. "Also Delma needs a sympathetic ear from time to time."

"Surely she has lots of women friends? Her own family?"

She knew she was pushing it, but the need to know gripped her.

He went quiet for a while. "Delma's family moved back to Italy when Delma was around your age. She loved it here, so she stayed. I think she was hooked on Owen even then."

"Now I suppose she's wondering what she got herself into?"

"She'll stay around," he observed briefly, picking up his wineglass.

"So what does that mean?" Eden asked in horror. "Has she threatened to leave Dad?"

"A threat only. A moment of despair and humiliation. What are your plans?"

She glanced briefly away. "I can never, never live in Dad's home. That's entirely out of the question."

"You say that now." His voice hardened suddenly. "If you wait a while longer things might settle."

She laughed in the middle of her anguish. "You're a clever man. You know perfectly well there's no chance of normality."

"I know equally well Owen won't allow his newfound daughter to get away," he retorted, narrowing his eyes. Reflected sunlight lit her skin. She wore a different dress, a summery white one. It made her look like a lily.

"Why do you hate me so much?"

He flashed her a brilliant look. "Don't be ridiculous. I don't hate you at all."

"But you find no joy in my sudden entry into your life?"

"Maybe I'm hurting too much," he said involuntarily, but it was too late to recall those revealing words.

"Are you trying to make me feel more guilty?"

"Are you? Marvellous," he mocked. "How come you lied so easily? How come you couldn't even warn me?"

"I told you. I couldn't go against Dad. I know it was wrong but why are you being so hard on me? Is it me or do you distrust all women?"

"Not until I met you," he scoffed. Why was he being so

hard on her? Hell, he didn't know. In a way it was an irrational reaction or he recognised a woman like her could hurt him badly.

"So there was never any thought of starting again?" she asked sadly.

"I invited you to lunch, didn't I?" He smiled at her. "It isn't as if I'm not fighting my disillusionment. It's probably because I expected so much of Owen and as an extension, you." You're the woman I wanted the minute I saw you, he thought, desire at full throttle even in broad daylight. My God!

"So what do I have to do to make peace?" she pleaded, looking at him over the rim of her wineglass.

"Just let me see enough of you," he said.

That made her extraordinarily confused. And for a moment blindingly excited, which was a measure of his powerful effect on her. She knew she couldn't withstand the force of this man's intentions. "Are you serious?"

"Oh, I am."

Another white taut smile as though in self-contempt.

"But we can't do it in one afternoon," he added smoothly.

"You're saying you think I should move north with Dad?"

He gave a brief laugh. "I know it sounds bizarre given my former defensive—"

"Censorious—" she was moved to point out.

"Attitude." He ignored her. "We should try being friends just to see what it's like."

She knew he was baiting her. "It could be a dangerous thing to do."

"It could," he mocked bitingly. "Good to do all the same."

Whatever note was in his voice it ravished her, proving beneath her coolness was a young woman's wild, beating heart.

CHAPTER FIVE

Six weeks later Eden found herself flying over the Tropic of Capricorn. Spread out below were glorious lyrical landscapes not to be missed. To the west loomed the rugged purple bastions of the Great Dividing Range. To the east, the Great Barrier Reef, one of the wonders of the world. Its coral ramparts, as solid as sandstone, followed the Queensland coastline for almost half its two thousand mile seaboard. From Capital to Cape. The Cape being Cape York Peninsula, a 100,000 square mile area of white beaches, aquamarine seas and prodigal jungle, off limits to most people, even at the turn of the twenty-first century. In between lay the lush coastal strip, the river valleys and rainforests, so vastly different in character to the sun-scorched immensity of the hinterland that lay behind the Range. That was the Outback. The Never Never. Cattle country. It was there the historic cattle stations spread their enormous "runs" to the Gulf of Carpentaria and the Northern Territory border. Sheep lands kept their distance fanning towards the central plains. A fabulous treasure trove of minerals lay everywhere beneath the ancient earth's crust, its wealth only now being tapped. She knew Lang's ancestral home, Marella Downs, was beyond the larkspur mountains. Maybe if she were lucky she would get to see it.

An hour into her flight and the captain announced they were over cane country. Sugarcane was the eternal presence of the tropical North. Hundreds of miles of ripe tall grasses, vivid green tipped with purple. It was a landscape of brilliant blue skies, green cane and bright red ochre earth, where the fallow paddocks formed a colourful mosaic. This was soil so rich almost anything would grow. Where the cane stopped the great mango plantations took over, the exotic fruits, the tea and coffee plantations, dairy cattle, stations that specialized in fattening beef cattle on the abundant vegetation. An astonishing number of small farms grew lucerne and other pastures for the herds.

The Tropic of Capricorn lay five hundred miles from Brisbane. It would be almost an hour before she arrived at her father's estate at Paradise Cove. This was to be a "visit" with the duration unspecified. Relations between her and Delma were by no means cordial. In fact they had scarcely progressed. They had only passing contact during the week Delma had remained in Brisbane before returning home to her small son, mercifully with no more talk of impending divorce. The fact was Delma loved her husband, as Owen had put it, right or wrong.

Eden had seen her father daily during his hospital stay, but neither of them got around to discussing Delma until Owen indicated, just as Lang had predicted, he expected Eden to come North with him as soon as he was discharged. Her own family home had been sold on her insistence. She and Redmond shared the proceeds. She had moved in with her grandfather to be of comfort only to find him inconsolable after her mother's death. As he would remain for the remainder of his life. He didn't try to dissuade her when she told him she had found a temporary home of her own, a rented apartment of good address. Maybe, eventually, she would buy it. For now her life was on hold, although she had gone back to work since. Redmond had resigned his partnership and gone off on his travels. The last postcard she had was from the city of Bandung in West Java. She had confided the true state of affairs to only her two closest girlfriends, knowing they would respect her confidence until the time for a full disclosure was right.

As for Lang? They had fallen into the habit of speaking over the phone. Sometimes twice a week. Odd calls. Calm and communicative on the surface, both filling the other in on what was happening in their lives, but disturbing never-theless.

She couldn't shield herself from the knowledge she was falling more and more beneath his spell. He interested, ex-cited and disconcerted her. Often she walked around in a half daze after a call. She feared that kind of magnetism, even as she invited it, continuing to hold these oddly intimate con-versations. It wasn't as though she hadn't had plenty of ad-mirers in her life. A few she definitely didn't want including two who had engaged her heart without moving her towards making a deeper commitment. Lang Forsyth was utterly dif-ferent to them all. No one had his charisma, that compelling magnetism, that built-in strength. In some ways he was as hard and brilliant as a diamond. She found that daunting and fascinating at the same time.

It was Lang who had urged her to accept Delma's invita-tion. Delma had made the first overture by phone, taking over from Owen to assure her they all wanted her to come.

"Roberto is very excited at the thought of meeting his sister," Delma had told her, with her very first show of gen-erosity of spirit.

It hadn't clinched anything for Eden. She dearly wanted to meet her little half brother but she knew Delma had more or less been forced into making that decision to please her husband. But always in the background was her ever-present desire to see Lang again. Not that anything could possibly come of it. He was a very complex man and he carried his own emotional baggage. As for herself? She was still suffer-ing much grief from the loss of her mother and self-destruction of her grandfather. She hoped with all her heart Redmond Sinclair would find the strength of purpose to throw off the shackles of the past. It would only take another woman. The right woman this time.

From the moment she felt the tropical sun on her face and head, Eden knew everything was different. The sights, the sounds and the smells. There was an enormous clarity and brilliance to the air. The Great Divide and the magnificent peaks of Bellenden Kerr and Bartle Frere reared thousands of feet into the air, providing a marvellous deep indigo back-drop for all the spectacular tropical flowering and vegetation. It was hot, of course. Very hot. And humid. She could feel tendrils of her long hair stuck to her nape. This was still the Dry. Christmas was a month off. But the Wet, according to her father was the best time to see the tropics. Then, new life seethed in the warm volcanic soils. Spectacular monsoonal storms loomed in from the Coral Sea; thunder rumbled along the range, its jagged peaks seared by great pyrotechnics of lightning. But the best thing about arriving on the verge of the Wet was the bush and the rainforest burst into prolific flower. The great poincianas turned into magnificent scarlet umbrellas, the yellow cascaras bloomed, the orange and scar-let tulip trees, the great mango trees and the ever-present brilliant parasite of the tropics, the bougainvillea; crimson, mauve, purple, white, along with bromeliads the wealth of orchids including the State emblem, the purple Cooktown orchid.

As Eden walked down the steps of the aircraft she could feel her own blood rise. A chattering crowd of tourists walked along with her across the tarmac. All of them were off to the beautiful Barrier Reef resorts. She felt such excite-ment! She so wanted this visit to be a huge success. She prayed Delma would have had time to relax her attitude and be friendly. But may be it was in the nature of things Delma would always be plagued by some jealousy. Only time would tell.

Eden saw her father the minute she walked into the ter-minal. He looked wonderful, fit and healthy, the joy of instant recognition paralleling her own. He was such a big imposing man that for a moment she didn't notice the handsome little boy, who was hiding shyly behind his father's long legs. Robbie! Her little brother. Eden's heart swelled with emo-tion. Robbie had a strong look of their father. The same head of thick dark curls and their father's fine dark eyes, down to

the shape and setting. Delma showed her Italian blood with
her colouring, glossy olive skin, a luxuriant head of dark hair,
which she had auburn rinsed, and large, flashing dark eyes,
but Robbie to Eden's eyes was much more his father than
his mother. And he was going to be tall. She, in fact, was
five seven, four inches taller than her petite mother had been.
Perhaps height was her only physical link with her father
apart from a few mannerisms.

Such was Owen's longing to see his daughter he reached
her flying figure before she reached him, gathering her into
a great bear hug.

"Eden, sweetheart!" he breathed. "I'm so thrilled you're
here."

She drew back a little, reached up and kissed his cheek.
"Dad! It's wonderful to be here."

"You had a good trip?" His eyes moved over her with
the greatest pleasure.

"Fine. Smooth as a pond. And who's this?" she asked,
joyously. Robbie was standing a foot from her staring up at
her with his big beautiful soulful eyes. "I know who it is,
it's my brother, Robbie."

Her hand came out to grasp the little boy's, instead the
grave searching look turned into a brilliant glow and the little
boy, with a look of excitement and delight suddenly rushed
forward and gripped Eden around the waist.

"Aren't you beautiful!" he cried. "Poppa said that you
were. I hope you're going to stay with us forever and ever."

Eden could feel the emotional tears spring to her eyes.
"Why that's lovely, Robbie." She smiled. "I know we're
going to be the greatest friends. I have something for you in
my bag."

"Have you? What is it?"

"Can't tell." She shook his hand. "It's a surprise. But I
think you're going to *love* it."

Owen was grinning delightedly at the both of them, his
expression full of love, and a certain satisfaction. "I'll leave

Robbie with you for a few minutes, Eden. I'll get the baggage cleared then we can set off home.''

''I'll take care of her, Poppa,'' Robbie said with aplomb, taking Eden's hand and leading her off to the rows of seats as though their common blood had provided them with an inbuilt affinity. ''Mamma's at home,'' he told her conversationally, after they both settled. ''She didn't want me to come so I had to do a little yelling. Poppa came home and told me to cut it out, and said that I could go.''

Eden's first reaction was a stab of dismay but she willed herself to ignore it.

''I'm so glad, Robbie,'' she said. ''I couldn't have waited a minute more to meet you. I think it's the most wonderful thing I have a brother. And you're so much like Dad.''

''Everyone says that.'' Robbie took his handsomeness for granted. ''Do you call him *Dad?*'' He turned to her, watching her closely.

''Of course I do. He is my father.'' Eden was matter-of-fact. ''I love calling him Dad.''

Robbie considered that, leaning forward in his seat with his elbows on his knees. ''I think I'll call him Dad, too. It sounds more grown-up. Do you want to hear me crack my knuckles?''

''Sure. Really that's very good,'' she said when he'd finished, then to distract the little boy in case he started again, asked where he went to school.

Robbie shook his head slowly, looking so much like Owen, Eden nearly laughed. ''It's a private school. Seymour College. It's really boring. Not my favourite place, even if us kids can do what we like. You know, go out and play instead of sitting inside having lessons. I'm a gifted kid,'' he tossed off and grinned.

''Are you?'' Eden's smile had real warmth.

''That's what they tell me,'' Robbie said. ''I can do pretty much everything they show me. I could read when I was three. I'm a whiz at sums. Just like Pop...just like *Dad*,'' he corrected himself. ''It was Mamma's idea. Dad wanted me to go to St. Anthony's for a couple of years. Then I would have to catch the bus. Mamma always drives me to Seymour and picks me up. She screams the place down if she can't see me straightaway. She screams so *much*. Once she told my teacher off something awful. Mrs. Spillane takes off every time she sees her. Mamma always thinks someone is going to kidnap me.''

Eden drew a sharp breath. ''Oh goodness, Robbie.'' She hadn't considered such a thing even when she knew her father was a very rich man.

Robbie laughed, an infectious little boy chuckle. ''Dad said anyone who stole me would soon give me back. Lang won't buy it, either.''

''The kidnapping bit?''

Robbie imitated a deep male groan. ''Lang told Dad, Mamma was into serious melodrama. I heard him say it. The minute they left the study I went to look it up. It means being *sensational*.''

Eden nodded. ''Probably it's because your mother loves you so much she gets anxious.''

''She says no to everything,'' Robbie said in a wry voice. ''Even kids' parties. Dad is the one who always says I can go. He says Mamma is keeping me from being an ordinary kid.''

Eden was saved an answer even if she could have found one; Owen joined them, wheeling Eden's luggage. ''What are you two chattering about?'' he asked.

''Nuthin','' Robbie laughed. ''Can I call you *Dad?*''

''Sure you can.'' Owen reached over and ruffled his son's head.

''No way I'm gonna go back to Poppa,'' Robbie said, jumping up and trying to take control of the trolley. ''I'm going to call you Dad just like Eden.''

Paradise Cove was an hour's drive in a big powerful Mercedes from the domestic airport. Eden sat in the back seat with Robbie. He had insisted she join him so he could hold her hand, and point out all the sights. They had left the main highway some time back, now they were climbing and the vistas of turquoise-blue sea and emerald off-shore islands were becoming more sweeping and spectacular. Lining the route on both sides like the most flamboyant of guardrails were the bougainvilleas, banks and banks of them, brilliant with colour: cerise and mauve. These were the originals from which so many hybrids had come. The hybrids though lovely in colour and relatively thornless couldn't match the original stock for sheer size and vigour.

"Look, Eden, you can see the house now," Robbie suddenly cried excitedly, leaning across her to point. "It's the big white one at the very top of the hill. Lang says it's like a great white heron came to rest. Lang is my godfather, did you know? Stop the car, Dad," he yelled. "Let's get out for a minute. There's nothing around."

Owen answered indulgently, pulling over onto the grassy verge. "All right, son."

Eden gazed for a long time, holding tight to her excitable little brother's hand. "How absolutely perfect."

Owen threw her a proud glance, thinking how much the exotic setting was suiting her. She looked as much at home as an orchid in the rainforest. "I gave the architect a free hand. Clever chap. Lang found him for me. I'd bought the piece of real estate years back when no one thought the North would take off like it has. I wanted the house to look gracious. I wanted it to look like it belonged, looking out over the blue sea."

"It's beautiful," Eden said, the shimmer of tears misting her vision.

"You won't ever want to go away, Eden," Robbie assured her, looking up into her face.

"Dad's here. I'm here. Uncle Lang's here. This is *home,*" Robbie cried with perfect joy.

Even at six, Eden noted, he had the perception not to include his mother.

*   *   *

It had to be one of the landmark estates in the area, Eden thought. She had seen some marvellous houses along the way, all overlooking the sea with its exquisite colourations. A deepwater marina was in evidence with the balmy back-drop of off-shore islands and coral cays.

"We have about seven acres," Owen told her. "And a private waterfront."

"We can play together on the beach," Robbie promised happily. "There's going to be so much to do. My school has already broken up. Other kids have to go to school for an-other week."

The house was set behind a high wrought-iron fence and a set of privacy gates allowing views of the beautifully land-scaped grounds, ablaze with colour; flowering poincianas and towering palms. To Eden's eyes the house was classic two-story Mediterranean. It could have clung to a cliff anywhere along the French Riviera or decorated a beachfront property in Florida, U.S.A.

Delma met them in the marble-floored foyer, a glamorous figure in a brilliantly patterned one-shouldered patio dress, her thick hair massed around her face with its dark honey tan.

"Eden, how wonderful to see you. Welcome to our home." She swooped on Eden, kissing the air to both sides of Eden's cheeks.

"It's very kind of you to have me, Delma," Eden re-sponded, realising Delma had felt compelled to establish this was *her* territory.

"Kind! Not at all. This is absolutely great. Roberto has been so excited." Delma's dark eyes fell not all that tenderly on her son. Robbie was still holding tight to Eden's hand as though he'd known her all of his short life.

"Eden's got something for me in her bag," Robbie in-formed his mother. "And guess what? I'm going to call Poppa *Dad*. Just like Eden."

"Oh I think you can call him Poppa for a while yet." Delma reached over and drew her son to her.

"I expect you'd like to be shown to your room, Eden,"

she said. "Actually it's a suite. I know you'll be very happy there during your stay."

"I'll have your luggage sent up, Eden." Owen turned to his wife. "Any word from Lang?"

"A brief phone call," Delma said. "I invited him to dinner just as you said. When Eden is settled we must throw a big party."

"That'll be great!" Robbie cried excitedly, fighting free of his mother's grip. "I won't go to bed."

"Oh yes, you will, my lamb," Delma said. "Remember what I told you now. You must behave yourself while Eden's here."

"He has been behaving himself, Delma," Owen said just a shade testily. "When you're ready, Eden, we'll have coffee or a cold drink in the solarium. Then I'll show you through the house."

"Lovely!" Eden answered blithely. "Coming, Robbie?" Her gaze swept up the spectacular floating staircase where she guessed the bedrooms would be.

"You betcha!" Robbie, a few feet away, rushed to her side. "I'm not going to let you go back to Brisbane," he cried. "You have to stay here."

"Thank you, Robbie." Eden smiled. She had already decided he was the nicest little brother she could possibly want.

As for Delma, she did her level best to relax and look happy. For all of her married life she had lived with the awful fear one day her husband would leave her and she would be alone. *This* when Owen had never remotely suggested he wanted out of the marriage. It was just that she knew he didn't love her. That made her feel bad. But he *did* love Robbie and this girl. And why not? They were his children. They had even taken to one another on sight. Delma knew her nerves would be screaming every minute the girl was around. Though she had gone dutifully ahead inviting Owen's daughter to stay, she had come face to face with the fact she couldn't wait for her to leave.

*   *   *

Woman-like Delma's sentiments wouldn't have come as a surprise to Eden but she didn't want to spoil her visit by giving it too much thought.

That evening she debated leaving her hair loose or gathering it into an updated French pleat. It was a beautiful night, but warmer and more humid than what she was used to. The house was air-conditioned but she had left her French doors wide open so she could revel in the great copper tropical moon and the exotic fragrances from the garden. They wafted in heady gusts with the slightest movement of the breeze. She could even isolate the myriad scents: red ginger blossom, jasmine, gardenia, the many-coloured oleanders, the Mexican white orange blossom, and the delicious waxy frangipani that flowered profusely beneath her balcony. Delma had spent a great deal of time consulting with their landscape gardener and the result was of great credit to them both. Not that they didn't have a head start with the spectacular flora and the growth patterns of the tropics. In the end she pinned her hair up, coaxing a few becoming tendrils to curl around her face and onto her bare nape.

Dinner would be at eight o'clock allowing Lang, who had only that day returned from a trip to Fiji where the company was negotiating to build a luxury resort, plenty of time to arrive. The thought of seeing him again had her quivering in anticipation. Fate had taken a long time to smile on her. She couldn't risk allowing herself to fall in love with a man who could very easily break her heart. And that was her perception of him. A dangerous, heart-breaking man. Possibly ruthless? Hadn't she experienced his icy contempt when he thought her aim was to break up Owen's marriage? He had also demonstrated where his loyalties lay. To his long-time friend, Delma, though she was certain there was nothing improper between them. But there hadn't been any of that marvellous compassion for her.

Be warned, Eden, she thought. This was a man who could deliver heaven or hell.

She stood in front of the long wall of mirrors studying her reflection. It was obvious from what she had seen of Delma that Delma loved clothes and wore them very well. Her own dress was a recent addition to her wardrobe. The cut was simple, a streamlined slip dress but the combination of pale blue chiffon with a turquoise silk lining was really beautiful, the turquoise silk defining the sweeping V of the neckline. She took pleasure in the fact she had given the young designer a flying start by buying and wearing his clothes at various well-attended functions. Her mother and Redmond had been invited everywhere. She had joined the list as a matter of course.

It was getting on towards seven-thirty. Robbie, as happy and excited as ever a child could be, had gone off, strangely unprotesting, to bed. Eden loved him already. He had accompanied Eden and their father on their inspection of the very large house and grounds, tumbling, doing somersaults, generally showing off, in the process thoroughly exhausting himself.

She stepped into her matching evening sandals then took one last look around the beautiful guest bedroom. It was as Delma had told her, a suite with a large dressing room and adjacent en suite. A spacious sitting room to relax opened out to the other side. It was all very comfortable and inviting, decorated in blues, yellows and white.

Downstairs the house was very quiet despite the soft sensuous music that was being piped through the home. Debussy. She recognised *Perfumes of the Night*. She already knew and had met the household staff of two, a husband and wife team of Italian extraction. The wife was an excellent cook and housekeeper—"invaluable with Roberto"—the husband equally invaluable as house manager and supervisor of the two full-time gardeners.

Probably Delma was still dressing, though they had agreed to meet in the library for a pre-dinner drink. Eden made her way through the living room, the main reception room, to the library beyond, pausing to admire all the beautiful paintings and antiques which had been mixed with wonderful contemporary sofas and armchairs on a large scale to suit the sheer space. Delma and her interior designer hadn't done things by halves, she considered. She couldn't imagine what the final cost must have been.

A soft smile on her face, she continued on to the library. The very last thing she expected was to come face to face with the man who was dominating too much of her consciousness.

Lang.

As she moved into the room he was striding out, a man on a mission, a faint frown between his ink-black brows, his whole demeanour one of dark, barely leased vitality. She found herself almost throwing up a hand; a form of self-defence against his challenging male aura.

"Eden!" He recovered first, his brilliant ice-grey glance leaping over her; shocking, thrilling, shaking her to the very core. He looked like a man in undisputed possession of her, his own world and every other horizon in sight.

She stood there, momentarily so transfixed she had to offer an explanation. "Lang! You startled me." Indeed her hand went to her breast.

"And you startle me afresh." His gaze shifting with shocking intimacy to her mouth.

She spent urgent seconds trying to hold on to her composure, only to have her efforts totally destroyed as he bent his marvellous dark head and brushed her cheek with his lips.

"So you're here at last!"

He spoke lightly, welcomingly, but he had her whole body throbbing. She knew she flushed. She could feel the heat in her cheeks. Still that sensuous *romantic* music spilled into the room.

"And I'm thrilled! It's all so beautiful," she replied. "So spectacular and exotic. It's been the greatest joy to meet Robbie."

Lang laughed. "He's a great kid. I thought I might hear him running through the house."

She smiled, too. "He's exhausted himself doing cartwheels in the grounds. Dad showed me all over the place. Robbie came, too." She paused to ask. "Were you off somewhere?"

"Actually out to the car. I have a little present for you. Something in the way of a peace offering. I thought I had it with me." He patted his breast pocket.

"Really?" She was charmed and amazed.

"Don't look so surprised," he said dryly. "I never dreamed when I found these things they'd be ideal for you."

"Now you've really got me interested." Pleasure flooded her.

"Come out to the car with me," he invited, swooping to take possession of her hand.

He moved like some sleek powerful cat. The warm pressure of his fingers around hers carrying like a current to every nerve.

"What a glorious moon!" She was panting a little. Not only from trying to keep up.

"Damn, I'm sorry." He halted, staring down at her. "I'm going too fast."

"Just a little." Her heart was beating so hard she thought it might fly out.

"Our copper moon of the tropics," he commented, lifting his face to the gold-dusted sky, certain he had never had feelings like this before.

They reached his car, a Jaguar. It was unlocked. He reached into the glove box, withdrawing a narrow box. "A new beginning," he said suavely. "Welcome to Paradise, Eden." For once his vibrant voice held no trace of mockery.

"Am I to open it?"

"Of course." He clicked his tongue. "Right here and now."

She didn't hold back removing the gold gift wrapping and exposing a dark velvet jewellery box.

"Go on," he urged, wondering how many thousand times he had thought of this girl. Sweet and exasperating in equal measure. He wasn't a man to be obsessed.

"I want to."

"Let's move closer to the light." He led her out of the shadows of the palms and onto the path. The sky was filled with a million glittering stars, the air redolent of gardenia and frangipani.

Excitement was invading every part of her. She went with him in a kind of mesmeric trance, her feelings intense. Inside the box was a beautiful necklace of modern design. She could see little V-shaped waves of silver set at intervals with be-zelled gemstones. She would have to get into the light to fully appreciate what she was looking at.

"Lang, this is lovely." She exclaimed, quite shocked. "I've done nothing to deserve this."

"Not so far, admittedly," he laughed. "But some things are meant to be. Your eyes are an almost identical colour. The stones are sapphires. My father used to take me gem fossicking when I was a boy. I found them all at a place called Anakie in South Queensland. Do you know it?"

"Of course." Even her voice trembled. "It's famous, but I've never been there. No one in my family ever did anything so exciting as gem fossicking."

"You can still do it," he told her carelessly, as though he had a trip lined up for the future.

"The stones I've had set are very fine. Violet sapphire. Like your eyes. I have others, green and yellow, a few pink and orange. I'll show them to you one day but these are the finest, most beautiful, almost tanzanite in colour. The setting is white-gold. Here," he said gently, impatiently, "give me that paper." He took the gold wrapping and ribbon from her, went back to the car, and threw it in.

"I want that," she told him breathlessly. "A keepsake." Two minutes back in her life and he had taken possession of her.

"Which just goes to show how appreciative you are." He walked back to her, a dynamic figure even by moonlight. "Put it on. I want to see it on you. You've even done me a great favour wearing that dress."

He turned her quickly so she couldn't see the leap of fire that came into his eyes. With her bare shoulders so seductively presented to him, her hair up, revealing her swan's neck, he was easily able to fix the clasp. A violent, totally rash compulsion to twist her around into his arms hammered away at him when he prided himself on his control. He wanted to find her lovely mouth, to let the desire that was in him out. He wanted to kiss every inch of her flower-like skin. Scores and scores of kisses, nibbles, tiny bites, tender and fierce. He wanted to feel her naked body beneath him, quivering, stirring, rippling to every stoke of his hand. He wanted her delicate nipples tight roses of sensation, in his mouth. He wanted to give in to this excruciating pressure, knowing if he ever did nothing would be the same again.

Goddammit! Why did passion have to come in the shape of Owen's daughter? he inwardly raged. One day it might be too hard to check. What then?

He could feel the hushed stillness in her body as though his desires were transparent. This he couldn't have. He removed his hands, deliberately keeping his voice low and casual. "Time to go back into the house, Eden. They'll be wondering where we are." He took her arm, taking care to hold it loosely, drawing quiet, regular breaths to try to rid himself of some of the sexual pressure.

"I don't know how to thank you, Lang. It's really too much." Despite herself she swayed towards him.

"Not at all." His voice made it perfectly clear it was a platonic gesture. "I'm only glad the sapphires have been put to excellent use."

"Then I'm honoured." She took his cue and answered brightly.

Once inside the foyer, Eden went to the tall gilded mirror above a mantle-topped console to take a good look at her necklace and admire it. It was even more beautiful under the brilliant light from the overhead chandelier. The little waves of white-gold gleamed, the sapphires, eight in number, all showing a wonderful depth of colour that enhanced her eyes.

His lean, wide-shouldered figure loomed up behind her. His skin was polished bronze from the tropical sun. The overhead light struck a near purple lustre into his crow-black hair. Against such darkness was it any wonder his brilliant eyes came as a mesmeric shock? Beside him though her own hair was as dark, her skin looked as pale as milk. He must have been thinking the same thing because he said, "You'll have to wear a hat every time you go out into the sun. And sun block."

"Don't worry." She nodded. "I always do. My mother had the same skin. Strangely enough it doesn't take a tan. Neither does it burn, not that I give the sun a chance."

"Then it's your great fortune to have skin like a camellia." He could have added, "It's also damned sexy," but he didn't. It just could be a colossal blunder to become involved with Owen's cherished newfound daughter. Feeling the way he did, the outcome could be unredeemable, irreparable damage. He'd, after all, plenty of experience. He thought Eden, beautiful as she was, hadn't. In fact her fastidious air stabbed at his heart.

As they walked back to the library he was silent and so was she. Both were aware of the intensity of the air between them. It ran like a turbulent current just below the seemingly smooth surface. Both of them, from the day of their meeting, had entered a kind of wilderness area. It was fascinating, to be sure, but with many a potential hazard and whitewater rapids.

The only thing it was really safe to talk about was the weather, Eden thought. Even with "family" she had to be so careful. Her relationship with Delma would never be close but they were trying their best.

Owen and Delma were waiting for them. Delma in rich yellow, her auburn-tinted hair gleaming, was sitting in an armchair sipping a glass of champagne. Owen was busy mixing a pitcher of martinis. Both looked towards them smilingly as they walked in the door.

"You timed that nicely," Owen called, his dark eyes full

of interest and humour. "I caught sight of you both disappearing into the garden."

"You're *too* good, Owen," Lang mocked. "You never miss a trick. Actually we went to collect a little present I had made up for Eden."

"A *little* present!" Eden scoffed. She went to her father and kissed his cheek. "It's this lovely necklace." She touched it with an elegant finger.

Delma rose immediately, full of curiosity. "Good grief!" she said, in apparent amazement.

"The sapphires have been waiting for someone with Eden's violet-blue eyes," Lang offered lazily.

"Lang fossicked for them when he was a boy." Eden turned full on to the light so her father and Delma could admire the beauty of the stones.

"But it's perfectly stunning!" Delma breathed in a kind of wonderment.

"You know I should have thought of something like this," Owen admitted honestly.

"Plenty of time, Dad," Eden joked.

"This is so nice of you, Lang." Owen peered at the necklace keenly. Openly admiring. "I really need my glasses. It suits you beautifully, sweetheart."

"Then I'm happy," Lang pronounced. "Those stones have been closed away for far too long."

"Couldn't you have given them to Lara?" Delma asked, mock-playfully. "Our friend Lara has beautiful blue eyes." Delma and Lara Hansen, one of Lang's long line of ex-girlfriends were good friends. Indeed Delma had been hoping for a match there.

"I don't think I've really noticed," Lang drawled. "How good are those martinis, Owen?"

"Not to worry, they're perfect," Owen laughed, his dark eyes warm, full head of dark hair swept back from his broad brow. "Just show the vermouth to the gin. Ice cold. A rub of lemon peel around the rim."

"Great!" Lang said. "I can feel all the little tensions of

the day dissolving.'' Even as he said it he could see Delma fighting mixed emotions. Delma had a proprietary streak. He knew she considered him her friend. Eden was entirely new on the scene. The outsider. He watched her drain her glass quickly and set it down. All of them were on a voyage of discovery, he thought. He only hoped all of them were going to cope.

CHAPTER SIX

THE days flew by. Incomparable blue and gold. There was so much to do and see. And the surroundings so different. Eden spent the first weeks of her stay in the most stimulating way. She had the warm loving companionship of her father, Robbie's bubbling high spirits, and the whole glorious district to see. If Delma didn't really want her at least she was making an effort to hide the fact. That brilliantly fine morning they were to visit the latest Carter-Forsyth enterprise, a country club development in an area of pristine natural beauty some thirty miles further up the coast.

"Lang's pet project," Owen told her as they drove along the spectacular coast road. "The centrepiece is the golf course. Japanese tourists love our golf courses and all our space. We had a top designer." He named a world-famous Australian golfer. "The course is almost completed. The clubhouse is up. Stunning if I say so myself. There will be luxury-built homes, villas, cottages. Most of them have been snapped up from the plan. I've left this one to Lang. He's absolutely first rate. A lot better than I am at handling people. Knows everyone just as everyone knows him. Goes along with being the scion of a great pioneering family."

"He did say he'd take me along on his next trip to Marella Downs."

"No kidding— Oh, you'll enjoy that!" Owen said, clearly pleased Lang had issued an invitation. "His mother is a lovely woman. You'll like Georgia, too, and her husband. Nice bloke. Lang worked like the very devil to buy back the farm. When I think about it, he doesn't get a whole lot of relaxation. Or a life of his own. He's only thirty-two. I forget sometimes. He's so mature about everything he could have

95

lived a lifetime. When I first met him he was absolutely driven to see his family back where they belonged. His mother especially. He adores her.''

"It's a wonder he isn't married," Eden said quietly. "Or engaged. He's a marvellous catch."

"Darn right!" Owen gave her a sidelong glance. "The young women around here surely know that. Lang's had his affairs along the way," Owen laughed. "He's definitely not a monk."

"What about this Lara, Delma keeps talking about?"

Owen snorted. "*Talk*. That's all it is as far as I know. Delma and Lara get along very well, that's all. They both serve on local committees. Lara's father owns a beef cattle stud. Brahmins. The Brahmin is at the forefront of beef cattle production up here in the tropics. There were many areas of the Outback where the British breeds couldn't survive. The Brahmins can. Hansen is a wealthy man. His father was one of the first to realise the great role the Brahmin had in the tropics. Lara is his only child."

"What's she like?" Eden asked, looking away from a scarlet silk-cotton tree alive with lorikeets after the nectar.

"Not a patch on you, sweetheart," Owen teased.

"You're biased."

"Put out a bulletin," Owen cried. "No, Lara is a very attractive and confident young woman," he continued slowly. "A bit uppity for my liking. Occasionally an outright snob, which you'll find Lang never is."

"And Lara was one of Lang's affairs?"

Owen gave his daughter another searching glance. "You're very interested, my darling."

She blushed. "Of course I am. Lang's your partner."

"Have *you* got your eye on him?" Owen questioned, sounding interested and happy at the thought.

"You sound like you'd be pleased?"

"You bet I would!" Owen continued emphatically. "I have the greatest liking and respect for Lang. He's everything I wasn't."

"Don't be so hard on yourself, Dad." Eden touched her father's arm. "We've found one another. I'm so happy."

Owen's deeply tanned face was full of light. "I don't want you to ever go back. You know that."

"It wouldn't work out, Dad," Eden gently said.

"It's Delma, isn't it?"

Eden flinched at the hardness of his tone. "Why, *no!* Don't think that for a minute. Delma is being very nice to me. There's the party tomorrow night. She's worked so hard to make it a success."

"Delma's good at that sort of thing," Owen said. "What she's *not* good at is opening up her heart. I couldn't bear it for her to chase you away."

"You're over-reacting, Dad." Eden hoped her protest wasn't overdone. "It's just I have a career. Even if it is on hold."

"But, my darling, if that's all it is I could get you into one of our top legal firms tomorrow. If you want a place of your own, I can find you one. Build it, for that matter. Whatever you say."

"Let me think about it, Dad." It came out as a soft plea.

"Sure, sweetheart. But please remember I desperately want to make it up to you for all the lost years."

Eden, the nature lover, was deriving enormous pleasure from her environment, the lush vegetation, the mix of spectacular trees, indigenous and exotic, the shrubs and palms that gave the tropics its distinct character. Twenty minutes later they were driving into the country club development, verdantly green and close to the water. As a setting it was brilliant, offering beautiful vistas. Eden looked quietly from side to side privately thinking the project was immense. It fronted onto the turquoise sea with miles and miles of pristine white beach. The eighteen-hole course seemed to go on forever. She could see lakes and bunkers taking shape, the vast body of emerald rolling turf that would make up the fairways and smooth greens. Beautiful towering native gums had been preserved not only for aesthetic considerations but to provide

shade for the spectators who would come to see the world-
famous players in action. Further back in the lee of a small
hill was a magnificent copse of magnolia grandiflora in full
flower.

Owen parked the car outside the clubhouse, asking one of
the workmen if he knew where Mr. Forsyth was.

The man signalled with his hand and a tip of his baseball
cap; Lang was in the clubhouse.

"Come on in, darling." Owen took her arm. "I didn't
come out here during my convalescence. Now I can see
things are moving along at a great rate. Not a darn thing
died, you know. Not those massive date palms flanking the
front gates, both replanted, many many small exotic trees.
Everything has thrived despite a few worries about initial
shock."

"And the hibiscus!" Eden exclaimed, her enchanted gaze
resting on hundreds of boldly coloured shrubs that were like
brilliant flashes of light. They had been planted all around
the perimeter of the classic all-white two-story clubhouse.
The size of the flowers alone was fantastic.

With a sense of excitement she accompanied her father
into the cool spacious interior, admiring the polished timber
flooring and the divided staircase.

They were halfway across the spacious foyer when Lang
appeared at the top of the first landing accompanied by a big
arresting-looking man of obvious Mediterranean heritage.
The man was carrying a sheaf of files, his voice audible as
he carried on his conversation with Lang. Both of them were
speaking beautiful, velvety, musical Italian.

The man switched to English immediately he caught sight
of them. "Owen, my friend. *¡Buongiorno!* How good it is to
see you!" He moved swiftly down the stairs, black eyes sparkling. "You look so much fitter than the last time I saw you.
In fact, my friend, you look wonderful and full of happiness."

The two men, much of age, went directly into a bear hug,
having developed a long and close friendship over the years.

"If I do it's because of this young woman," Owen said, turning to Eden with evident love and pride. "Eden, this is my great friend and our chief architect for the building development, Bruno Canturi. Bruno, this is my beautiful Eden I've told you about. We've been parted for all of her young life but we'll never be parted again."

Bruno gave her a swift appreciative assessment. "*¡Molto bella! i vegle occhi!* The beautiful eyes." He bent over Eden's hand. "One must hold on to these wonderful moments. Life can be so full of heartbreak. I am very happy to meet you at last, Eden. My wife and I wouldn't miss your coming home party for the world."

"I'm so glad you're coming," Eden responded instantly to his charm. "The clubhouse is very fine," she said, looking around her with sincere admiration.

Lang, having held back, now joined them. "Bruno is the finest architect in this part of the world," he said, clapping one hand to Bruno's broad shoulder. "Without doubt one of the top men in the country."

"I can see that." Eden smiled. "I love what you've done already, Mr. Canturi. Your design embodies the whole ambience of the tropics."

"*Grazie.*" The architect looked pleased. "But you must call me Bruno, I can't have a beautiful young woman calling me Mister."

"Then it's Bruno," Eden said with a charmed expression.

Owen, eyes smiling, spoke warmly. "If you have a few minutes, Bruno, I'd like to talk. Lang keeps me up to date on all developments but I'd like to hear and listen to what you've got to say. Everything looks to be well ahead of schedule?"

"A lot of work must be completed before the rains." Bruno gave the small warning. "But, yes, Lang and I are very happy with the progress so far."

"Why don't I show Eden around while you two have your talk," Lang suggested, giving Eden his total attention.

"Great idea." Owen smiled over his shoulder at his partner.

"Shall we start with the grounds?" Lang asked Eden smoothly, a curve to his generous chisel-edged mouth.

"I'd enjoy that." She inclined her dark head. "Will you be here when we get back, Bruno?" she asked.

"*Molto piacere,* but my days are too short!" Bruno exclaimed, one hand extravagantly on his heart. "But we are so looking forward to your party."

"So am I!" Eden's fine delicate features lit with unfeigned pleasure. "*Ciao!*"

"*Ciao!*" Owen and Bruno responded together.

They were out in the brilliant sunshine and Lang immediately asked, "Where's your hat?"

"It's a long time since anyone has had to check up on me." She tipped her face to gently mock him.

"I'm only trying to protect your beautiful skin. Surely you bought one?"

"Yes, I did. The last thing I want to do is invoke your displeasure."

"Really?" He gave her a lazy smile laced with some inner amusement.

They had reached Owen's car. Eden opened the rear door and removed her hat with its wide floppy brim.

"Put it on," he ordered briefly.

She gave a helpless little shrug. "Have you decided to play big brother?" She settled the hat on her head.

"What do you think?" His silver eyes were brilliant, taking possession of her in their slow scrutiny. "Now that's what I call a beautiful hat. Functional, too. Women should wear big romantic hats more often. You look like you've stepped out of a painting." His smile tautened.

Beneath the creamy curving brim of her hat decorated with full-blown pink and cream roses, her eyes glowed with a blue-violet fire. Today she wore her hair full and loose the way he especially liked it. It fell heavy and shining about her shoulders, the dark silky strands reflecting light. If he'd spoken love's language instead of hiding forever behind secure and intricate defences he'd tell her he'd found her unforgettable since the first moment he'd laid eyes on her. But then that would have exposed the follies and obsessions of the heart.

"Why don't we take the buggy?" he suggested, guiding her towards a golf buggy parked in the shade of a billowing golden cane. "It's quite a distance we'll be covering."

Eden allowed herself to be led away, realising with some trepidation she was falling in love with this man. It was too easy to see why. Probably she would meet a few of Lang's ex-girlfriends at the party. She knew for a fact Delma had invited her friend, Lara, whom she seemed to view as faultless....

"I don't understand how Lang has waited so long to pop the question," Delma had confided, rolling her eyes. "They make a great couple. Both from landed families, of course."

Of course.

"How are you getting on with Delma?" Lang asked as if he were reading her mind. It brought her out of her slight reverie.

"Fine," she said brightly. "Delma's making every effort to make my party a big success. I do appreciate it."

The sun glanced across his carved cheekbones. "Delma has a lot of experience in that direction. I'm asking more on a personal basis."

"What do you want me to say, Lang? I know Delma is your friend."

"And *you* aren't?" He started up the buggy, taxiing it onto the driveway.

"Maybe the next best thing." She spoke quietly, looking away across the sweeping vistas and shining man-made lakes.

"Which is?" He cast her a slashing glance, lightning-quick.

"*Owen's* daughter," she shrugged.

He digested that in silence, then observed, "You've succeeded in making him very very happy. Whatever else he's

been, Owen hasn't been a happy man. An impressive man
and a brilliant entrepreneur, but there's always been this great
sadness at the heart of him. Now that's all over.''

"It's over for me, too," she answered slowly. "In some
strange way, I've been yearning for a true father all of my
life.''

"But now you've found him, you don't intend to stay with
him? That is what he so desperately wants.''

A whole world of regret flashed through her. "As I told
Dad, it wouldn't work out.''

His expression tightened. "I hope there was no hint Delma
was to blame?''

"Of course there wasn't!" She flashed him a look of sudden anger, her camellia skin deepening with a flush. "Now
why would you say that? No, hang on a minute. Of course
you'd say it. You've been programmed not to trust me.''

He turned his head fully to confront her. "I really can't
agree with that, Eden. It's just that I have the terrible feeling
Owen would choose you over Delma every time.''

It was so much her own fear she over-reacted. "Please
don't be so absurd. Dad wouldn't do that. It would be un-
believably cruel.''

"Are you so sure?" he questioned in a dark-tinged voice.

"I would hope he would never do that. Marriage is sacred.
I've seen too many lives destroyed when it hasn't been regarded as a sacrament.''

"So you empathize with Delma?''

"Of course I do." Her heart was hammering. "She's had
a rough deal. And I'm a woman, too.''

"A very fascinating one." He sighed as though that alone
presented an insurmountable problem.

"I wish you were a kinder man." She half turned her body
to look off to the sequin-splashed blue sea.

"What then? Would you have an affair with me?''

Her blood pressure soared. "I don't have affairs I'm
afraid.''

"You must be due for one," he said. "Not a silly little affair. A grand passion."

"You must think I'm starved of affection."

He filled his eyes with her beauty, her natural fragrance an intoxicant. His own heart was pumping fast.

"If you were, it doesn't show. What does show is your very fastidious, look-but-don't-touch virginal air."

The air around them was aromatic with morning and the scent of the sea. "How extraordinary you should think that. I've led the normal life of a successful professional woman."

"So you've had your love affairs?" He flickered a shining glance.

"That happens." She wouldn't look at him. "I have to tell you, Lang, I don't usually answer questions like this."

"But then you and I were thrown headfirst into some form of intimacy."

"I suppose it is a bit like that."

Moments passed. Fraught moments, when neither seemed inclined to continue.

"Let's get out and walk for a while," he said abruptly, steering the buggy towards a stand of eucalypts.

"Fine by me." At this point the best thing she could do was put a little distance between them. Her emotions were cranked up enough. Around him they were running mad. She suspected she would always feel particularly vulnerable around him. As soon as he brought the golf buggy to a halt she slipped out of her seat, making towards the beautiful stand of eucalypts that created such light and shade. It was very hot, the surrounding areas of green bathed in an immense pool of golden sunlight. She was wearing a cool rose-pink cotton sundress with a full skirt and spaghetti straps but still she could feel the beads of perspiration gathering between her breasts.

"What's the hurry?" He caught her up with his purposeful, elegant stride. "You'll have to learn not to rush around in the heat."

"I'm sure I'll get used to it." She wanted to push him

away. She wanted him to touch her. "After all Brisbane is subtropical."

"You seem upset?" He bent his sleek, dark head to study her face beneath the curving brim of her hat.

"You're not a comfortable person to be around, Lang." The tension in her throat made it hard to swallow.

"Well," he said, almost nonchalantly. "I am to most people. I admit *we* have a few problems."

That was it! The two of them. "I'm astonished you could admit to having a problem." She struggled to keep her cool but between the heat of the sun and the blood heat his presence generated she was fighting a losing battle. "But then, you're very macho, aren't you? Very assertive and aggressive."

"Hey, hang on." His lean strong hand folded onto her bare shoulder. "Next you'll be telling me you dislike me intensely."

"It wouldn't be difficult," she burst out. Only it was too easy to fall in love with him.

He removed his hand in silence. "I think you've got many reasons for finding me...difficult..." he answered. "It wouldn't take a Freud to trace it back to our first meeting. I deeply regret having misjudged you, Eden. On the other hand I found your secrecy somewhat intolerable."

She experienced a keen sense of hurt that showed in her eyes.

"But you knew the reason."

"And I'm forced to accept it. You can't let your father run your life, that's all."

She pushed her riotously curly hair from her flushed face. "So it's Dad now?"

"Don't misunderstand me. In Owen's eyes you're his most perfect creation."

"You mean he doesn't remember he has a beautiful little son?" Her skin was alight with a fine glow of inner anger.

He shrugged. "I'm not saying Owen doesn't love Robbie.

Of course he does. He's always ensured Delma and Robbie have everything they want and need. Except for his time."

All around her was confusion, resentment, hurt...passion. Where was her habitual cool?

"Aren't you being disloyal to Dad?" she queried, her voice edged with censure. "Your mentor and partner?"

He didn't look away from her transparent face. "I don't think so. I'll say it in front of him any day. In fact I have. I just want to be sure you're seeing it. Turning your back on things doesn't help."

"I'm going home."

She looked to him like an exquisite, wounded child.

"You don't have a home anymore," he gently reminded her.

"I still have my grandfather."

"Maybe, but you don't know your father as well as you think, Eden. He's a complex man. Having found you he isn't simply going to let you go away. Certainly not to your grandfather. He hates him and that won't change. I'm sure Owen has offered to find you a position in a good legal firm. If he realises you won't be all that comfortable staying at the house, he'll build you one close by. Owen is a very persuasive and forceful man. He will find a reason to keep you here, as any father would."

"But you want me to go? Let's really have this out."

"Of course I don't!" was his emphatic reply. "I understand perfectly why Owen needs you. He loves you. Finding you has made up for all the misery of his past."

"Yet you feel something bad is going to happen? I have to rely on your psychological analysis?"

"I didn't say that. I'm only asking you to steel yourself for a few problems. Owen will be changing his will. He's already spoken to me about it. I expect—"

"He certainly hasn't spoken to me," Eden cut in. "I don't need money."

His handsome mouth compressed. "It can cure a lot of life's ills. In view of what you suffered yourself you're more than entitled to your share. Life can turn on us.'' He would never forget how he had to work to rescue the family.

''You think Delma will be fearful on account of her son?'' Eden asked carefully, staring away at a glittering lake where a blue crane, a brolga, had alighted. ''Who, incidentally, is my little brother?''

''*Half* brother. He's Delma's child. Jealousy is taking over a bit too much of Delma's life. I suspect she has worries about Robbie's inheritance as well as the security of her own position. She must be wondering where the bulk of the money is going. Her nose is thoroughly out of joint on any number of fronts. As you're so intelligent and intuitive I'm sure it comes as no surprise to you.''

''Doesn't money create a problem,'' she said wryly. ''I'm more interested in family. I know Delma will never see me as part of her family. But I've only come for a holiday. Tell me, Lang Forsyth—'' she tilted her head ''—since you've firmly injected yourself into my life. What do *you* think I should do?'' she challenged.

''I don't like fighting with you,'' he said, giving a deep sigh.

''I don't like fighting, either,'' she replied as though there was no love lost between them. ''Please answer the question.''

His eyes turned brilliant and hard, like precious stones. ''Simple. Get on with your own life. Move out of the house when the holiday is over. You won't have to search for a job. Owen could find you one in half a minute. For that matter so could I. The same goes for a place of your own. You won't be alone. You'll see your father and Robbie often. You'll make a whole lot of new friends. You'll meet a lot of young people at the party.''

''I have friends,'' she said sharply. ''I have a good job.'' And indeed the freedom to come and go as she pleased.

''In your grandfather's firm. What about Sinclair?''

''I don't think he'll be coming back.''

"You're not *sure*. He might feel a whole lot better in a year. I expect people have to be told something?"

The understatement of the year. "It seems to me your real worry is Delma."

"Good God!" He struck his temple with a kind of despair. "These days Delma is a real pain in the neck, but I can't help feeling *sorry* for her. She's up against the wall."

"Can't she search inside herself for some compassion?" Eden countered. "For that matter why can't you? You don't want to understand. Or forgive." She was more and more agitated, his whole aura overcoming her.

"Eden, I'm sorry!" He put out a hand in apology. "Please don't run away."

But she was already on the move, unable to quench her nerves. She was still in a state of trauma. Trying to absorb her mother's premature death, worst of all handle the grief. It was a great joy, certainly, to be with her father and Robbie but she had the feeling Lang Forsyth was right. Her father would exert his powerful will. He didn't want her to go away. He had suggested a course of action only that morning. It was possible he wanted in the most benevolent way to take control of her life.

As for Lang Forsyth! She couldn't bear the tempestuous feelings she had for him. He made her come alive, but there were so many raw edges she wanted to resist him.

She let her flying feet take her further into the thicket of eucalypts with their lovely nostalgic aromas. Soon she would have to stop and confront Lang. And there was the rub! She wanted him to take her into his arms, to cover her mouth with his own. She wanted to lie against his chest. She wanted him so *close*. Her habitual composure was fragmenting into shards of emotional glass. She was, finally, in a man's power.

She didn't see the wallaby that broke cover of the trees, scenting her approach. When she did lift her head its sudden appearance, however unthreatening, gave her such a fright she let out a strangled little scream. It caused a chain reaction. Instead of hopping away the wallaby, unpredictable like its big brother the kangaroo, bounded towards her, eyeing her with curiosity, suspicion and alarm. She was confused, her feet rooted to the ground. When it was less than two bounds away Lang closed in, driving it off with a vigorous wave of a branch.

"I'm sorry. That was stupid." She was apologetic, embarrassed. "I know they're harmless."

"Sometimes they *aren't!*" His voice was like flint. "We haven't had any wallabies in so close. That fellow will probably make it back to the bush."

She lifted the hat off her head and fanned her face, struggling to regain a semblance of normality. "That's enough excitement for today."

He watched her, unable to keep his eyes off her, full of hard aches and driving longings. "Is it?" He was mad to kiss her. Why the hell not? There had to be the time for living dangerously.

He saw the swift understanding in her beautiful sapphire eyes, the start of violent excitement in her slender body as realisation hit her. This had to happen, he thought. He reached for her, his touch electric, drawing her hard up against him, so she was standing, light-limbed and trembling in his grasp.

"You're exquisite!"

He could even taste her. He savoured one long moment before he claimed her sweet, tender mouth. He didn't have to search for it. It was there, as though she offered it to him because she knew resistance was futile? Or because desire as powerful as his own was over-riding everything else.

All the passion he had suppressed came drumming to the fore. He brought up his hands, held her face, before descending into kissing her; mouth and body hard, his kiss was deep and ravenous like a starving man presented with luscious fruit. He knew he should keep a rein on his feelings but control had simply abandoned him. He couldn't contain his feelings. They were fierce, agonizing, full of a wild splendour. The tiny moan that escaped her only served to fan the flames...

The green and gold world around them faded to nothing. There was only this searing ring of fire...

When he finally released her, how young and poignant she was revealed to be. Not a woman of the world at all. Beautiful and vulnerable, she appeared little more than a girl. His hands moved to her delicate bare shoulders, his muscles tense as he kept them from straying to her breasts. From his height he could see she wore no bra, or the bodice had some lining to it. All he was aware of was the impeccable sculpture of her satin curves, the rose tips aroused and like berries. What had gotten into him? Sexual obsession? His body was taut like a high-tension wire. He was crazy for this girl. He didn't even think he could wait much longer before he made love to her. He wanted to draw her into a world of limitless dimension. It was too late to be careful. For once in his life he was in much too deep.

He was older by some eight years. Far more experienced. He knew instinctively she had much to learn though she stole his every breath. Her eyes flickered, then opened wide. The pupils were dilated, the irises, a deep purple.

"That was bound to happen," he rasped. "I've wanted to kiss you since the moment I laid eyes on you."

She was so shaken for a moment she couldn't find her voice. "Is that what you call it, a kiss?" she managed.

"You think it was much more?"

"More like a takeover." She ran the tip of her tongue over her sensitive lips. They pulsed from the pressure of his. "I don't know what else to say."

"Maybe it was in the nature of a warning," he suggested. "Kisses like that can lead anywhere."

Right to his bed.

She didn't answer, but looked away, trying to retain a veneer of composure.

Lang bent and retrieved her hat. "We'd better get going," he said quietly. "Owen is taking us to lunch."

"Yes, I know." She allowed herself to glance at him briefly. Those silver eyes were pure voltage. "I suppose I don't have a scrap of lipstick left?"

"You wouldn't know it," he examined her. "Your mouth is as red as a rose. But you could come here to me," he said, with a return to his normal sardonic tones.

"You think you can control me anytime?" Spirit flashed in her black-lashed eyes.

"I don't think I'm controlling you at all," he told her bluntly. "You wanted to be kissed as much as I wanted to kiss you, so don't give me the *ingénue* routine. I only meant there's a leaf in your hair."

"Oh, I'm sorry." She went to him, feeling foolish, dipping her dark head. Half hidden in this grove of trees the atmosphere was immensely intimate, yet so sexually claustrophobic her body was reacting in a kind of panic. She wasn't any innocent maiden but, God, he made her feel like one. In fact, he was playing her like a flute.

CHAPTER SEVEN

No ONE was better at throwing a good party than Delma, Lang thought.

Everything was memorable, the mix of people, the level of enjoyment, the music, the flowers. So Delma had a lot of money to play around with? Still, not everyone in their moneyed circle did it half so well. The food was wonderful, so was the wine, there was champagne throughout except for a few extraordinary people who didn't care for bubbles.

He was deep in conversation with a friend, talking about his favourite topic of the moment, the country club, when he sensed Eden had walked back into the living room. It was filled with people obviously in a great mood, but they all took time off to stare.

Eden was a dream walking. When she had first come down the staircase to greet him time had stopped. She looked fantastic, incandescent, as beautiful as he knew she would be on this night of nights. He was thirty-two years old, well experienced with women; highly successful at everything he did; yet he had never suffered such powerful reactions. In a way they had become dangerous intrusions into his ordered life. Much too quickly Eden had woven her spell. He was beginning to wonder if she had picked him as her victim? Women were capable of being goddesses.

He'd been a little late arriving having flown back from a quick trip to Marella to see his mother, so there was already a crowd. He spotted many of his friends as he glanced into the huge brilliantly lit living room. The house was abuzz with laughter, conversation and lovely relaxing background music. It all faded as Eden walked towards him, her eyes seeking his. He was virtually spellbound like some poor fool without defences.

She wore her hair long and wavy, fuller than usual, her unique eyes full of sparkle and welcome for him. He couldn't look away from her though he heard someone calling his name trying to attract his attention. To no avail. There was a delicate flush of excitement on her cheeks. She wore his sapphires around her throat. They looked possessed of an uncommon radiance. Sapphires and diamonds were at her ears. They were a gift from her father. Owen had told him all about it and how he proposed to surprise Eden the night of the party. Her evening dress was short, showing her beautiful, delicate legs. It was made of some exquisite filigree silver lace that reminded him of something. Some beautiful thing tucked away in his tangle of memories, something his mother had worn perhaps? The dress skimmed Eden's body and left one shoulder bare. She came to him a graceful creature yet he had the curious feeling she was the moth that was walking to the flame. There was still enough of him left to be dangerous and he was letting her get far too close.

"It's lovely to see you, Lang," she said as she approached, her smile so full of joy and excitement he would have liked to capture it on camera forever.

"I'm sorry I'm late," he apologised as she joined him. They had gone right past any ordinary polite greeting. He bent his head and kissed the satin cheek she presented, enchanted by her fragrance. "You look a dream."

"Why, thank you." Pleasure shone in her blue-violet eyes. "You look marvellous, too." She took him in at a glance. "Dad told me you'd flown over to see your family? I hope they're well?"

"They're fine. I told them all about you which means you'll be getting an invitation very soon."

She was clearly delighted and surprised. "To see Marella. To meet the family? How lovely. I'll look forward to it." She glanced past his white dinner-jacketed shoulder towards the scene in the living room. "Everyone seems to have accepted me."

"Be certain of that," he said just a shade sardonic. "You're Owen's beautiful only daughter restored to him..."

Hours later, his friend, Harry Richardson was among those staring, in the process losing track of their conversation. "You have to forgive me, Lang," he said, in a slightly hoarse, confidential voice. "But who is she really?"

Irritation etched lines around his mouth. "What the devil are you talking about, Harry, she's Owen's long-lost daughter."

"I know, my boy, I know. But God what a story! She's absolutely beautiful, isn't she? And so cultured. I'm quite impressed. In fact I'm devastated that I'm an old man approaching fifty."

"With a wife and four kids," Lang reminded him laconically. "Eden looks what she is. A young woman of excellent background. She comes from a legal family. She is herself a lawyer."

"Clever girl!" Harry chortled admiringly. "Legal family, eh? What firm?"

"You're very curious, aren't you?"

"Everyone is!" Harry maintained very dryly, eyeing Eden's progress across the room. It was slow as many guests stopped her, genuinely enthralled, wanting to get to know her better. "I love the dress. She seems to be heading towards you, my boy. You're such a devil with the ladies. They're all drawn to you. Too much success for your own good, I'd say."

"Thanks, Harry."

But it was Lara Hansen who was most desperate to find Lang alone. She took the opportunity to swoop on him before Owen's love child could fight her way across the room. Of course they had been introduced on arrival, Lara was quite intelligent enough to realise she had better make a big fuss of the young woman who had so suddenly and dramatically entered the Carters' lives. She knew all about Delma's private feelings. She and Delma had grown close. Though there were seven years between them, they shared the same interests, and physical pursuits, sailing, playing tennis and golf. Delma was too anxious about too many things not to confide in her. Lara knew Delma had been fearful for a long time something would occur to drive a wedge between her and her husband. Now came Owen's grown-up love child out of the blue!

She might look like butter wouldn't melt in her mouth but according to Delma the girl was working behind the scenes to exert her growing influence on her father. In reality Owen begrudged Delma nothing but Delma had confided she was worried Robbie was going to lose much of his inheritance. It didn't matter so much about her—or so she said—but Delma was becoming really depressed about what changes Owen would make to his will. Not that anyone would associate Delma with depression looking at her tonight. She had gone overboard on her dress, the ultimate in glamour in her favourite scarlet.

When Eden paused to speak to a group of guests, Lara made her move, reaching Lang and locking her fingers around his arm. She was almost *sick* with wanting this guy but no matter what she did, and she had turned all her feminine wiles on him, Lang managed to keep their relationship fairly casual. It all made for a deeply unsatisfied state.

"So when are you going to dance with me?" she asked, with a provocative smile, looking up into his handsome, enigmatic face.

"Lara, how are you?" Lang immediately turned away from Harry who wiggled his fingers at Lara and moved off.

"This *is* a party," she pointed out with a deliberate pout of her full lips. "You're not supposed to talk business."

"How do you know I was talking business," he teased.

"That's the centre of your life, isn't it?"

"I'm starting to realise it is." His vibrant voice turned wry.

Lara's blue eyes swept the room. "Owen's love child appears to be winning everyone over," she said lightly, not missing Lang's sudden frown. He could look so severe sometimes.

"I don't think Owen would appreciate that term, Lara, any more than I do. I wouldn't like Eden to hear it, either."

Surprised by his tone, which bordered on curt, she backed off. "Well I'm awfully sorry if I've offended you." She lightened her pressure on his arm. "I was speaking facetiously. Personally I think she's absolutely lovely. I'm sure we'll be good friends. I want Delma to bring her over to visit us."

"That'll be nice." Lang swallowed down the white lie, regretting the sharpness of his tone, but he was sick of the bitchiness.

"I can't say I blame Delma for being a little worried about the state of the marriage though," Lara continued, unaware.

"What is that supposed to mean?" Again Lang showed his impatience.

"Why don't we go out onto the terrace?" Lara urged, already beginning to move. "It's a gorgeous night. Delma and I are friends. It's only natural she confides in me."

"So is it acceptable for you to pass on her confidences to me?" Lang asked, nodding at several of the guests.

"Don't be like that, Lang," Lara pleaded, moving onto the softly lit terrace. "Delma adores Owen, you know that. I know it's odd but Delma has never felt really secure. Now I suppose she had—reasons?"

"I take it you mean Eden?"

"You're as observant as they come, Lang." Lara gave a faintly bitter laugh. "Don't tell me you haven't noticed how much Owen dotes on his daughter? He behaves as though *she's* the centre of his life. Not Delma or Robbie. I suppose Owen is acting out of a sense of guilt."

Lang was angry and didn't care who knew it. "Lara, I don't want to have this conversation."

She stared up at him in the golden glow. "I understand, but you can see I don't want my friend hurt in any way. Delma tells me Eden is very friendly when Owen is around but it's a different story when they're on their own. All the warmth evaporates it seems."

Lang kept his voice deliberately low. "Now *that* I don't believe. Delma is misrepresenting the situation for her own ends."

"Please, Lang, it's not as though she's complaining, but she does need a sympathetic ear. Somehow Delma's got it into her head that Eden is trying to penetrate the family in such a way Delma's own position will be usurped."

Lang walked a little way down the terrace, the exterior lights flickering through the tall golden canes that stood in pairs flanking the French doors. He was trying hard to control his anger, caught unawares by Lara's sudden onslaught. He could hear her high heels tapping on the terracotta tiles as she ran after him.

Let her.

The night was tropical and the sky full of a billion stars. The scents of the garden in this area were richly fragrant, with a top note of gardenia. Gardenia, the delicate fragrance so like Eden's skin. But it was Lara not Eden who put a staying hand on his arm, her voice filled with pleading and a touch of pure fright as if she realised she had set their long-standing friendship back.

"Surely we can *talk?*" she protested, feeling jealous and singularly unloved. "We've known one another forever. Why are you so angry? What is this girl to you?" Lara's full shapely bust, accentuated by her sequined strapless gown, rose steeply. "I hope she hasn't gotten to you, as well?"

God how that jarred! "Just a moment, Lara." He found himself pressing his lips together. "This is a party. It's been given in Eden's honour. And here you are, after telling me you hoped you and Eden would be good friends, warning me her middle name is opportunist. Isn't that what you're saying?''

How clearly he put it. Lara sighed painfully. ''You're merciless when you get started, Lang. Sometimes I wonder why I care about you so much. I thought you owed me some loyalty. Delma, too. She isn't lying. She's said there's much to like and admire about Eden, but she's genuinely worried about what is happening in her life. It's not a crime for Delma to share her worries with me. And me to share mine with you. We're all close friends.''

''You're not doing a bad job of it, are you?''

Even in the semi darkness she couldn't miss his caustic expression or the angry flash of his eyes.

''I'm not trying to belittle Eden,'' she pointed out, absorbing the very unpleasant fact that Eden had made quite an impact. ''That would be a bad thing. There are causes for everything. Eden must have felt deprived. Now that she's found her father she wants to become a very important person in his life.'' Perhaps the most important person in his life? she left unsaid.

''She already is,'' Lang informed her.

''Do you have a different slant on this?'' she appealed to him, lifting her honey-blonde head. ''I assure you I want to listen to everything you say. I have great faith in your judgment, Lang.''

''Then you'll report back to Delma,'' he questioned cynically. ''I think I need to keep this to myself, Lara.''

''Now you're angry with me,'' she said tremulously, dipping her head. ''Change can be terrible, Lang. Please reflect on that. It's not all that hard to understand both Delma's and Eden's responses. It was everything to do with Owen and the battle to share his love.''

''Let's leave it there, shall we?'' Lang put his hand to her shoulder, his voice as gentle as he could make it. ''There's always a huge problem with money. But Owen is a very generous and fair man and he's in his prime, with many more years left. Surely Delma's concerns are a bit premature? Let's go back into the house.''

"Then you can dance with me,'' Lara said throatily.

Inside the spacious solarium, which had been cleared for dancing, Eden was encased in the arms of a big, burly, rather sweet young man called Gavin Lockhart when Lang and his friend Lara Hansen made it onto the dance floor. She could see the excitement on Lara's face, the look of adoration in her clear blue eyes. Eden found to her astonishment she had to look away. Jealousy snaked through her, startling her. It was a new, unwelcome experience and it complicated life. Lang looked marvellous tonight, silver eyes blazing against his tan, very elegant in formal dress, his dinner jacket, like a good many of the other male guests, white, which looked so good in the tropics.

"I think I've had enough for the moment, thank you, Gavin,'' Eden said gently, having endured jarred toes caused by Gavin's joyous abandonment to the dance.

Gavin's good-natured face fell. "Already?''

"I've been dancing for ages.'' She smiled. "I would like a glass of champagne though.''

"Of course,'' Gavin beamed at her. "I'll get it. Don't go away.''

"I won't be far.''

In fact she made her way out onto the terrace, resisting several more offers to dance on the way. It was blessedly cool in the night air. She drew in a quiet breath, hoping a young man she had danced with previously, now speaking to a very attractive girl over by the playing fountain, would not come down to her. Her head ached just a little. She had been watching what she drank, not risking the chance of becoming intoxicated although the champagne flowed. This would be her third glass of champagne. It was almost time for supper, which she knew would be sumptuous. Delma had done everything in her considerable power to make this night a great success. She had even taken Eden to a favourite boutique where she'd bought her dress, struck by the quality and range, blushing a little when Delma told her there was plenty of money in the North and plenty of women with the where-withal to indulge expensive tastes.

The night sky looked wonderful, the Milky Way a curving river of diamonds. Eden broke off a scented gardenia, pressed the velvety petals to her lips. She was full of ever-unfolding emotions that perpetually kept her off balance. She had barely seen enough of Lang in the crush. It was hard to accept he'd had a full life of his own that excluded her, but clearly included other women. Why not? With that male sensuality. His friend, Lara, in her sexy gold-sequined satin dress couldn't hide her feelings for him.

She heard footsteps along the tiled walkway. They were coming towards her purposefully. It was probably Gavin, with her glass of champagne. She turned quickly, her smile fading.

"Oh, I thought it was Gavin," she said, excitement rippling.

His smile was sardonic. "I think Gavin can spare you for twenty minutes or so. But here's your glass of champagne."

"Which means you took it off him."

"How else could I get to see you?" he mocked. "You're a great success this evening."

"I can't remember all the names. But all very nice people."

"So here you are with *me*."

However he shaped the words they filled her with a desire that had the potential to destroy her. Excitement surrounded them like a heat haze surrounds fire. She sought escape by sipping at her wine, feeling its delicious cold tingle in her mouth. "I met your friend, Lara."

"You make that sound like Lara and I are an item. We're not."

Tell *her* that. "She's very attractive. I'm surprised you couldn't remember the colour of her eyes. They're a bright clear blue. But that wasn't true, was it?"

"No." He gave a brief laugh. "I was attempting to head Delma off. It's fairly obvious Delma would have liked us to become seriously involved."

"And you're not?" She set the champagne flute down gently on top of the balustrade. She was intoxicated enough.

"I have to say I've been toying with romance up to date, Eden," he admitted, keeping his tone light and amused. "But then I have an excuse. I've been much too busy to make a big decision."

"You'll have to soon," she dared to taunt him.

"Really? Any suggestions?" He looked down at her, driven by a desire that rolled in like a pounding surf.

"Like the good girl I am, I'll keep out of it." She glanced away across the floodlit gardens, lapped in fragrance.

"Which is a shame really. I could let myself fall in love with *you,* only it would constitute too much of a crisis. As it is, I'm surprised I haven't simply picked you up and carried you away."

Colours seem to burst in front of her eyes. Though there was self-mockery in his tone it was apparent some powerful emotion was lashing at him. She, too, felt the sting.

"To where?" she whispered, wanting nothing more.

"Oh, far into the enchanted night," he said.

She had dreamed of this.

A night bird dipped so low with a sheen of wings her lips parted in a startled cry. Lang lifted a long arm to frighten it away.

"You're nervous." He could see she was trembling.

"So you've noticed? I think you like it this way, with me, off balance."

There was a long silence broken by the crackle of flame.

"I remember the last time I kissed you," he said.

"The *only* time." He had made the soul float out of her body.

"Extraordinary." He leaned back against the balustrade. "I feel I've known you all your life. That, I *don't* understand. Now what are you doing with that flower?" he asked in mock exasperation, allowing his hand to take it from her, bewitched by its fragrance.

His height and the width of his shoulders seemed to blot out the sky.

"I suppose we should go in." This was pleasure but also fraught with dangerous high tension.

"It seems a bit like that," he said, feeling a hunger that devoured because it could not be satisfied.

They had scarcely begun to move when they heard Delma's voice. She sounded slightly rattled, as though something wasn't going to plan. "I know they came out here."

Eden very nearly moaned while Lang gave a muffled, "Hell!" His white teeth clicking in irritation. "Now we have the girls in hot pursuit."

"Delma and your friend, Lara," she whispered, having caught the gleam of Lara's satin gown further down the terrace.

"That's what they think." In a swift, deft motion Lang locked a purposeful arm around her, pressing them both to the wall, their bodies screened by the large handsome fronds of the golden cane.

Eden found herself pinned to the point of rapture! His hands rested on her hips as he pulled her even closer, fingers flexing over taut flesh and bone.

Eden stood motionless, trembling. Sexual excitement she couldn't stop was pouring into her. Her blood scintillated, her heart beat madly. She never knew it was possible to feel like this. She couldn't even trust herself with this man.

Another world away, Delma and Lara continued their low discussion about where Lang and Eden might have gone.

Surely they could *see* her she was so alight? She felt like a creature of air and fire. Lang's creature. Eden knew she made a small, incoherent sound, seduced the instant he put his hands on her. Not fighting him but wanting him.

Full of his own jagged need, Lang sought her breast, laid claim to it, his hand shaping the high tender curves, moving back and forth, feeling through his fingers her fluttering heart.

Delma's low-pitched voice was still audible, but he was too far gone to care. This woman was everything he had ever wanted. It was as simple as that.

His touch was scorching, burning them both. So scorching Eden thought her skin might actually emit a sizzling sound. She could feel the hard thrust of his arousal, and her body moved in spontaneous response, so he half lifted her from the ground to draw her even closer.

God, where was this going? Was that her ragged sigh, breaking…breaking…

Hush!

It was to die. Or swoon away with ecstasy. His fingers were teasing her molten nipple, his other hand smoothing her body with a marvellous pressure, hot, sweet and fierce. She had to arch back against him, biting her lower lip in a futile effort to restrain herself.

"To have you like this always," he whispered.

The captive moth now an exquisite butterfly.

While they were lost in the purple shadow of seduction a distance from them Delma burst out in frustration, "They must be in the library. They can't have got lost!"

Lang grunted deep in his throat. He pushed Eden's hair aside, kissed the nape of her neck. He held tight to her swaying body letting his senses run riot. Such skin. Such silk. He wanted his mouth over hers, *passionately,* but at some point they had to go back inside with all eyes on them.

Suddenly there was silence at the other end of the terrace. The music wove in and out. "I think they've gone," he murmured, thinking he couldn't possibly prolong this exquisite torture before he bore her away.

"They're really starting to hate me," Eden lamented, understanding that was so.

"Nonsense. Everyone loves you." Now he had to act. Last chance. He turned her to him, forcing back the violence of his feelings, the uproar in his body. "Delma will get a hold on her jealousy. Give her time."

"Not to mention…Lara," Eden murmured shakily.

Lang continued to hold her, delighting in the closeness of her body. "Lara is just plain envious." He turned his head to look the far length of the walkway. "We can slip in through Owen's study," he suggested. "It's open. You can rest a minute."

She would have to. She felt feverish, nerves humming like live electricity wires. Distractedly she smoothed her lace dress over her hips. "I can't believe the things you do." He had peeled her like a peach.

"When I'm being so very, very careful with you?" he mocked, lifting her hand to his mouth. "That tide of yearning wasn't all mine, Eden." The rush of radiance.

"I know," she confessed. "But I didn't want…I didn't mean…"

"Liar," he said gently.

It was difficult to get through the rest of the night after that. Owen gave a speech over the lavish supper. It was an emotional speech that brought the sting of tears to quite a few eyes. None of these people had had the faintest idea Owen had a daughter until very recently, and now they could see what had been the cause of the deep sadness they had only sensed. Owen was to be congratulated. The near unanimous verdict was that Eden was simply beautiful and a great pleasure to meet. The same number of guests hoped she would remain in the community and not go back to Brisbane. Surely Owen, clearly doting on his newfound daughter would never allow it?

Though Delma's dark eyes smiled and Lara maintained her warm friendliness, Eden knew neither woman was sincere. If they could arrange it, both would have her disappear in a puff of smoke. She had upset their world.

It was two o'clock in the morning before all the guests had departed. All except Lang who generally stayed over on these occasions. He had long since had his own guest room, which made it all so easy.

"It was a lovely party, Delma. Thank you so much," Eden

told the older woman gratefully. They were all about to retire. Owen in the greatest spirits, standing in the living room, his arm around his daughter's narrow waist.

"Thank you, too, Dad." Eden reached up to kiss his cheek, touching his other cheek tenderly with her hand. "It was absolutely wonderful. And thank you again for my beautiful earrings."

"The start of a collection," Owen promised her, studying them with delight. "They look beautiful on you, as does Lang's wonderful necklace. Oh, God, sweetheart, this is really happening, isn't it?" he asked, not bothering to hide his emotion, and it was as though a dam had collapsed. "It's not some heart-breaking dream, is it? I used to have them, you know."

"It's real, Owen," Lang said, touching his friend's shoulder.

"I'm afraid at the same time," Owen admitted slowly.

"Why, Dad?" Eden stared up at him sudden anxiety in her eyes.

"I worry that you'll go away." Owen brushed the long beautiful hair from his daughter's cheek. "I love you."

"Don't get over-emotional, Owen," Delma warned, as if her husband had some heart condition. "You're embarrassing Eden, too."

"No, no, he's not. I'll always be there for you, Dad."

"Not *there*, darling," Owen shook his head. "*Here*. This holiday will soon be over. I don't want a temporary daughter."

Delma intervened quickly. "Owen, dear, Eden must be exhausted," she said, giving Eden a sympathetic smile. "She was the centre of attention all night."

"Of course, I'm sorry. Go to bed, darling. Have a good sleep. Tomorrow I thought we might all go out on the boat. Suit you, Lang?"

"Fine." There was warmth in Lang's voice. "By the way on this night of nights I have a suggestion for the name of the country club."

"It looks like absolute heaven," Eden said, sincerely. Her eyes made one final sweep over Lang's tall elegant figure. He had removed his black tie, and his white collar was open, exposing the dark gold of his throat.

His expression was near to triumphant. "That's it exactly. Lake Eden. Do you like that?"

Owen's dark eyes sparkled with surprised delight. "Lake Eden?" He tried it on his tongue. Came to a conclusion. "If you ask me it's perfect."

"I rather liked Emerald Cove," Delma said frankly, referring to a former suggestion.

Owen looked at her in faint exasperation. "Lake Eden it is. Right, Lang?"

"Like you, I think it's perfect. What about you, Eden?" He stood looking at her with a strange intensity.

Her eyes held a trace of embarrassment. She loved the name, but surely Delma had a right to her choice? Sometimes her father could be much too crisp with his wife. Too authoritarian. Maybe it was the age difference. She felt for Delma.

"Well?" Owen prompted as Eden remained silent.

"It's wonderful, Dad. I'm honoured." She went to him, kissed his cheek, standing on tiptoe to do it, then she moved towards Lang who thrilled her by putting out his arm and gathering her to his side.

"Lord, what a night it's been!" he said, wishing with every fibre he could simply carry Eden off, her beautiful dark head a weight against his heart. But he had nowhere to take her but the guest room in her father's house. Hell, hell, hell, he thought thickly. He willed himself to let her go and briefly kissed her cheek. All pure. My God! He walked to the bottom of the staircase, taking a last long look at her as she said goodnight. Kissing her was such a powerful punishment when he was desperate for so much more. Owen would probably have him in jail if he knew his thoughts.

*   *   *

In the soft opulence of her bedroom Eden too was lost in her own erotic dream. She undressed slowly, lingeringly, her body reliving deeply those minutes on the terrace when their passion had burned like a flame. She had wanted Lang to take her back to his room. Take her to his bed. She knew he would be the most marvellous lover. She touched the tips of her breasts, fingers stroking. Her nipples were so sensitive they still retained a residue of that fantastic sensation. She wondered what it would be like to have his hands on her naked. Utterly wonderful!

She walked over to a bowl of red roses, sank her face in their fragrance. She had the most powerful urge to wait until the household had retired then find her way along the hallway to the west wing. Her ache for him was so bad it amounted to real pain.

How would he greet her, the man with the silver eyes?

Would he look at her as though she was just another woman he could easily seduce?

Would he look at her with love and desire? Her fingers trembled as she stared down at them. She bit her lip realizing there was no cure for what she had. Her long hair fell loosely over her shoulder and she threw it back impatiently. He'd felt as she did. She knew it. Her skin still carried the scent of his. Her mouth still bore the imprint of his. His caressing hands had left a searing trail of stars.

Eden moved to the doorway, looked up at the huge copper moon. The moon of the tropics.

Dream of me, she whispered. As I'll dream of you.

CHAPTER EIGHT

EDEN awoke with a start. Someone was tickling her ear. She stared up into a dear little face.

"Robbie, love!" She sat up quickly in bed, feeling the least bit giddy. "What time is it?"

"Sunup," he said cheerfully, climbing into bed beside her. "How was the party?"

"Wonderful, wonderful!" She drew him into a cuddle. "You saw the guests arrive?"

"Some of them. Mummy made me go to bed. She's always fussin'."

"Well it was getting late. But there are some lovely things to eat left over and Dad is going to take us out on the boat later on."

"They're asleep." Robbie flopped onto the pillow. "Mummy saw me but she told me to go back to bed. She was cross."

"I'll bet! It's only six o'clock."

"You're not tired, are you?" Robbie turned to stare at her appealingly.

"Strangely enough, no. Not now that I'm awake."

"Did Uncle Lang stay over?" Robbie asked hopefully. "He always does."

"Yes, he did."

"Oh great! He lets me do things. I wish I had a Dad like that."

Eden felt a state of dismay. "But you love Dad, Robbie?"

"Sure I do but he's always busy. He never seems to take much notice of me."

"Well we'll have to slow him down," Eden said. "Dads have to do things with their kids."

"Right-on!" Robbie put up a hand to slap a high-five.
"What say we go for a walk on the beach? I could bring my
beach ball."

"Great!" Eden pulled herself up. "Go get dressed and
meet me back here. I'll throw a few things on."

"Cool!"

Morning was a sunburst of beauty. The breeze soft and warm,
the sparkling sea, blue in all its facets; royal, turquoise, sapphire, transparent aquamarine in the shallows. A feathery line
of white surf broke on the shore and the water was surprisingly cold on their bare feet. The horseshoe-shaped curve of
the cove was bordered by a wide stretch of pure, unspoiled,
almost bone-white sand, behind that ranks of tall coconut
trees their large fronds making a clacking noise as the wind
sailed through them.

In the distance she heard music. Rock music.

Eden felt so happy she started to dance. Robbie joined in
with all the joy only children possess. "Isn't this great! Isn't
this great!" he cried, racing up to hug her before resuming
his dance.

Seagulls circled and milled. Robbie clapped his hands,
calling to Eden to witness the progress of some hunting por-
poise further out in the dazzling blue water.

"Look at them. Up and down. Up and down. They won't
hurt you. Neither will the dolphins. We never see sharks."
He raced to the water's edge, cheeks glowing, the breeze
whipping through his curls.

What a dear little boy he is, Eden thought with a lift of
the heart. My brother. She would have given anything for
Lang to be there on the beach with them. It would make
things perfect. He made her feel so romantic she marvelled
at it. Though she had gone to sleep breathing his name, his
phantom lips against her skin, she had sunk into a dreamless
sleep as though her feelings were too perilously intense and
had to be shut down.

She stared back at the house. He should be up soon. Hopefully he would catch sight of them from his bedroom balcony. She could see herself waving to him, in delight.

Join me. Join me.

Robbie called to her, bringing her out of her reverie. She had been led to believe Robbie had been spoilt by his mother. Perhaps he was. She knew Delma was more than a little phobic about her son's safety, but essentially Robbie was a very nice, good-hearted, child who was coming to confide in her. She took his comment about their father not giving him enough time very seriously. Owen, before she had come into his life, must have been a lonely being, wary of letting others into his heart though it was obvious he thought the world of Lang. But that was another man. A partner. An equal. Owen had to find more time for his little son. Also he might start telling his wife he loved her. That would be a start. It had struck Eden forcibly that insecurity was at the root of Delma's problems. She could empathize with it.

But after last night, her thoughts couldn't stay away from Lang. She seemed to be powerless against him. She curved her fingers around a beautiful smooth shell. Was that a good thing to feel powerless? To give one man so much dominance? Yet she was permitting it, aware she had fallen passionately in love. Separation from Lang would be a traumatic experience. In a way, more traumatic than intermittent separations from her father and Robbie. She seriously doubted her ability to take any more heartbreak. So why had she laid her heart wide open? It was so strange, when for so many years of her life she had depended on no one. Not her despairing mother. Not her grandfather. Certainly not Redmond Sinclair. Maybe she had been starved of emotional attachment.

Lang was such a dynamic person. And so *sexual*. Her cheeks blushed hot. Going beyond caring about anyone or anything would have been unthinkable for her once. But then she'd never been trapped in such rapture before. She'd been kissed, caressed and touched of course. She wasn't a virgin. She'd had two fairly serious relationships, truly caring at the

time, but in retrospect…unmemorable. Even to kiss Lang
brought such completeness, such intensity. Nothing held
back. It was extravagantly seductive. So much so she was
frightened she could be getting herself into something so far
over her head it might damage her. She had always been a
whole person, her objectives clear, whether her studies or
relationships in general. She had never played at romance.
Her two relationships had advanced considerably before she
consented to intimacy. Now she was confronted by a man
whose sexuality was so much a part of his personality it
overwhelmed her. That put her at some peril. She'd seen how
much Lara Hansen cared for him. Probably Lara had shared
his bed, but she hadn't stolen his heart.

Did he have a heart to steal?

They stayed on the beach for anything up to an hour. She
wasn't sure. She wasn't wearing her watch. She'd barely had
time to pull on a pair of shorts and a T-shirt before Robbie
had raced back into her room, similarly attired except for the
red baseball cap which he wore, like the other kids, back to
front.

It was hunger that finally got him. He ran out of the water,
whooping for joy.

"Cake," he shrieked. "That's what I want. A piece of
party cake."

"You can't be serious?"

"Yes." He beamed at her and squeezed her hand. "Isn't
this lovely to have a sister? I can tell you everything. Please
don't go away."

"Back to Brisbane you mean?"

Robbie yanked on her hand. "It's much better when you're
here. Dad laughs a lot."

Eden tickled him, picking on a popular TV ad. "That's
because he's getting in touch with his feminine side."

That struck Robbie as very funny. He kept laughing while
they climbed the long flight of steps that led to the home
grounds.

After such fun, on such a piercingly beautiful day, Eden was stunned when Delma came flying through one of the French doors, demanding to know where they had been. Delma was even moved to get hold of Robbie's small shoulders, giving them a shake. "Don't ever go anywhere without telling me," she cried, wheeling him around to face her.

"Delma, we were only down on the beach!" Eden protested, positioning herself beside Robbie. "If you'd walked over to the cliff edge you could have seen us clearly."

"That's beside the point." Delma's voice was pitched high enough to bring her husband out of the house, followed by Lang, both men looking incredulous.

"Delma, what's the matter?" Owen loomed up, a big man looking fiercely impatient.

"I've had such a fright," she said, turning around to face him. "I expected to find Roberto in bed. Eden had him out on the beach without telling me. I would have thought after last night she would sleep in."

"Well she didn't," Robbie shouted back, catching his mother's tone. "Eden is my friend."

"Be quiet, Roberto," Delma chided.

Robbie retaliated by stamping on his mother's toe. "Let go."

"How dare you!" Delma slapped him in outrage, little more than a tap, but the child dissolved into torrential tears.

"Look I'm sorry about this, Delma," Eden apologised, thinking Delma's behaviour was way over the top. "Robbie came to my room to see if I was awake. I was, so we went down to the beach where we've had a very nice time. Surely that's no cause for alarm?"

"It's perfectly normal," Owen said wearily. "Only Del likes to work herself up into a lather the instant Robbie's out of her sight."

Delma stared at him mortified. "I would have expected you to leave a message with Maria, Eden. She's always up and about."

"I'll do it next time, Delma, I promise."

"Leave Eden alone!" Robbie stopped his tears to bristle. "She's my sister."

It was Lang who shushed him. "Come on, Robbie, what say I give you a piggy-back into the house? You must be ready for breakfast?"

"What I want is party cake," Robbie told him, diverted to happiness.

"Yeah, well." Lang swung the child onto his shoulders. "Come with us, Eden." His voice was carefully controlled, but he was angry with Delma. She'd have to get her paranoia under control. Eden had gone very pale. That disturbed and upset him.

"You go. I'll be in presently," she said. "I want to admire the sea vista." She knew Lang was aware Delma had upset her. She could see the fine blaze in his eyes.

"I think I'll give my boy a good talking to," Owen frowned. "I can't have him actually attacking his mother."

"Honestly, Owen, he only stood on my toe." Delma sprang to her son's defence.

"The next time it might be a kick in the shins. I plan to head it off. Coming?" He reached out an imperative arm to his wife.

"In a moment. I want to explain myself to Eden. She doesn't know what it's like to be a mother."

"While you're at it explain what else is bothering you," Owen clipped off.

While her husband moved off Delma turned to Eden. "I'm sorry if I upset you, Eden. It's just that I always exercise caution with Roberto."

"*Over*-exercise, Delma," Eden suggested quietly, thinking she should be frank. "Forgive me for pointing it out. Had it been Lang who had taken Robbie out it would have been perfectly all right. But you resent me. I know you've been doing your best to hide it but I can see it gnawing away at you."

It was the time for truth. Both women knew it. "Wouldn't you be resentful in my position?" Delma asked.

"I've thought through your point of view, Delma. I know your fears, but the reality is you don't have legitimate grievances. Dad wasn't unfaithful to you. He was in love with my mother long before he ever met you. It's not like I'm trying to divert his love and attention. I love Robbie already. And this is only a *holiday* for me!"

"You don't expect me to believe that." Delma looked off to the sparkling blue sea. "You know it. I know it. You're staying. Don't think I haven't noticed this little thing you and Lang have going."

"What Lang does isn't your business," Eden pointed out.

Delma had the grace to blush. "So he's sexy, vibrant and handsome. Don't you realise you could be just another experience for him? Over before it's begun."

"Again none of your business," Eden said quietly. "I'm a woman, twenty-four years old. I'll make my own mistakes. Let's forget this conversation."

Delma bridled. "You must consider I'm older than you, and a whole lot wiser. Also I've known Lang a long time. I can give you advice. All the women fall for him. Lara has had more success than the others. I don't want to see Owen's daughter hurt." Neither did she want to see Lang and Eden forge a relationship with Owen's blessing that might threaten Robbie's future. So many fronts to cover!

"Leave it to me, will you, Delma," Eden said with exaggerated calm. "I don't need your advice."

"I suppose you intend to go to your father?" Delma questioned, a strange appeal in her eyes.

"Calm down, Delma. I'm not going anywhere," Eden said. "You don't need *me* to put Dad off side. You're doing the job well enough yourself."

Eden was sitting on a stone bench looking sightlessly out to sea when Lang quietly joined her. "What was that all about?" He reached for her hand.

"You're the expert on Delma," she returned.

Lang studied her profile, seeing clearly she was upset.

With no make-up—she didn't need it—her hair wild and loose around her face, her light-limbed body clad in a casual top and brief shorts, she looked about fifteen. "We all know she's a little paranoid about Robbie," he commented dryly. "She never lets him out of her sight."

"A *little* paranoid." Eden pulled her hand away impelled by the warring forces within her. She began to curl the ends of her hair abstractedly. It was a habit she'd long since grown out of.

"I think it will come to a head pretty soon." Lang flung both his long arms over the back of the bench, his tone wry. "Owen has had enough."

Small wonder!

For a moment they sat, side by side, in silence.

"I've said all along I don't want to come between them." Eden, on this beautiful morning, was unable to lay down her tension. "It's obvious Delma is terrified I will."

"She has an insecurity problem. But why the hell talk about Delma? I'm more interested in us." He looked her directly in the eyes so she flushed. "We made a little love last night, remember?"

"I remember." Indeed she would never forget.

"Did you dream of me?"

She gave a soft sigh. "I sensed you near me every second until I shut my eyes."

"And?" His eyes sparkled in the morning light.

"Then I fell into a deep dreamless sleep."

"So you wouldn't have heard me if I came knocking softly on your door?" He picked up her hand and pressed his mouth to her wrist. "I want you fiercely."

"For how long?" she asked, plaintively, perversely influenced by Delma's remarks. "I think I need a little protection from you."

He laughed briefly. "You surely can't be suggesting I'm some kind of a predator?"

"I know you're capable of taking a woman captive." She flushed and looked away.

"And you fear that state?"

"Yes I do," she said passionately, her intensity even shocking her. "You've gained a lot of ascendancy over me in a very short time. You sometimes behave as if…"

"I own you?" he asked, putting emphasis on it.

"Yes," she said huskily, while shockingly tears sprang into her eyes.

He looked at her with anger and compassion in equal measure. "I realise Delma has upset you but don't do this," he warned. "I can't take your tears without wanting to gather you up. It was no game of seduction last night, Eden, if that's what's causing this anxiety state. I stopped playing games a long time ago."

She ran the back of her hand over her eyelashes. "I'm sorry. I admit I'm off balance, but too many things are coming at me at once, Lang," she endeavoured to explain. "I'm trying to work through my relationship with Dad. I haven't *had* a father for the past twenty-four years. It's wonderful how easily we've fallen into one another's arms—the same goes for Robbie—but Robbie's only a little boy. My father is a grown man. A powerful man. And deep down, a very complicated man. A man who has lived largely in the past. Emotionally anyway."

It was his own perception. "You mean he continued to stay in love with a woman who only existed in his memory?"

Eden nodded, for a moment unable to speak. "There are some lines in poetry—I can't remember who wrote them—about who stayed in the imagination most. The woman won or the woman lost."

"I'd be damned if I'd lose the woman I loved," Lang said in a voice that was loaded with passionate force.

"That's *you*," she retorted. "Your personality. You're the quintessential all-conquering *male*. Dad has near wasted his life living with a dream. It's so sad. I don't really wonder why Delma feels so insecure. In fact, I sympathize with her to some degree. Dad isn't exactly a doting husband, is he? Then there's you."

Lang half turned to look at her. "I knew I'd come in for my share of criticism. You make meeting me sound like you've been plunged into fire."

"Fire is a good example." She moistened her mouth, tasting salt. "I need time, Lang. I'm used to being cool not frantic. You go right beyond any boundaries I'm used to."

"You mean your own sexuality comes as a big shock?"

"Yes." She licked her dry lips. "Isn't that pitiful?"

He reached out to tuck a long windblown curl behind her ear. "It's perfectly understandable. You're troubled enough. And you're right about Delma, in case you don't think I'm on your side. She does see herself in jealous competition with you for Owen's love. You can't solve that no matter what you do and neither can I. The only one who can bring Delma peace is Owen. He made his choice. Delma is his wife. She in turn might be doing herself a huge favour if she stopped screaming and yelling all the time. As for us, I don't think I was putting so much pressure on you, Eden. What I feel for you is far more than sexual desire if that's what's frightening you."

Brilliant lorikeets swirled in the air, before dive-bombing the grevilleas. Eden turned her head to look at him. He was so handsome and vital, carelessly elegant in a pearl-grey cotton sweater over a pair of taut jeans. His hair, like hers, was tousled by the wind, one glossy lock rested rakishly on his forehead. She had to admit that she loved him. The first passionate love of her life. "It is and it isn't," she said quietly. "I'm sorry I'm so intense about everything, but you have such an element of excitement and danger about you."

He rolled his eyes satirically. "Oh, come off it, Eden. I don't accept that. I think what you're talking about is emotional risk. You find me as compulsively attractive as I find you, but you're frightened to show too much of yourself. That's okay." He shrugged a nonchalant shoulder. "I've led a guarded life myself. Forming an intimate relationship is a very serious business. You can't do it if you're determined on keeping your distance. Which is what I've done by and large. Becoming a big success has assumed too much importance in my life."

"But you're not obsessive like Dad. Or in the *way* he is. You did most of it for your family."

He raked a hand through his wind-ruffled hair. "I wouldn't allow my mother to suffer. Losing my father was devastation. I couldn't change that for her. Losing Marella was a mere setback after that, but I could and did effect change."

"And this is love," she said. "Your mother must be very proud of you."

"She is and she always makes that abundantly clear to anyone who will listen," he said a little wryly. "I come from a loving family. It's a good start in life."

"I believe the best," she answered quietly.

Driven by compassion, he reached out and ruffled her curls much as he would Robbie's. "So okay, young Eden, relax. You look about fifteen anyway. We can draw back from any deeper relationship if that's what you want. This is a fragile time for you. I'm quite happy to play big brother."

She began to smile. "As if that were possible!"

"Don't be so certain of that!" His silver eyes mocked her. "I see your point. Things have been happening too damn fast. Even for me."

She nodded as if in agreement, but one part of her was contradicting the other. "I don't think I want to go in to breakfast," she said, uncertain of the atmosphere inside.

"No one is going to bother you," he told here reassuringly. "I'm hungry. Let's eat something on the terrace. If you feel like escaping for a while, a few days, a week, you could always visit Marella. Now the party is over, you can expect my mother's call."

"That's very kind of her." Pleasure lit up Eden's small features.

"She is kind. As for me. Ah, well..." He smiled at her enigmatically, extending a hand-up. "By the way, do you ride?"

She nodded enthusiastically, her eyes full of delight. "I

was lucky enough to be put on a pony before I could even walk. My mother and grandfather loved riding for relaxation. Both of them used to take me aboard. I went to the local gymkhana, then a good equestrian centre.''

"You sound quite nostalgic." He continued to hold her hand as they walked back across the emerald-green lawn.

"Those were the good times." She released a poignant sigh.

"Then you'll love Marella," he promised. "I'll speak to Owen. You'll find he'll be delighted to let you come."

Blue sea, blue sky and the dazzling brightness of glorious sunlight was undiluted by cloud. Being out on the water shocked Eden out of the morning's upset, acting like some miraculous balm on her mood. A light trade wind was blowing across the deck where she and Lang were lying, he in full sun; she mostly shaded. The sheltered waters around the off-shore islands were incredibly luminous, close to the colour of a gas flame and as smooth as glass in the calm conditions. The surface glittered with a billion needles of sunshine. Even now with her eyes closed and hidden by sun-glasses Eden was able to ''see'' Lang clearly. She only had to move scant inches for her fingers to touch his bare tanned shoulder. She was taking everything in through her senses, for all her talk about backing off, by far the stronger part of her clamoured for him.

He had a superb body, beautifully made. It resembled an athlete's body, his wide shoulders tapering to a narrow waist and long lean flanks. Even in a pair of board shorts he looked so good he made her mouth go dry. Her father was up at the helm, thoroughly at home on the water. Delma was in the galley with Robbie, deeply absorbed in the preparation of the lunch. She had subtly excluded Eden as she did with every-thing but Eden was determined not to mind.

"How's it going?" Lang raised himself onto one elbow, staring down at her. She was right when she said her white skin didn't take a tan or burn. It looked like unflawed porcelain, emitting light.

"Isn't this simply glorious?" she breathed, taking off her sunglasses to smile at him. "I feel so peaceful." Not strictly true, when all her meditation included him.

"Would you like to go over to one of the coral cays?" he asked, looking away from her breasts.

"I'd love to!" She'd been half reclining under the umbrella, now she sat straight. "That beautiful little one over there." She pointed to the nearest coral cay in the area. Native casuarinas grew along the strand line along with the picturesque pandanus with its segmented orange fruits and characteristic prop roots. A grove of coconut palms waved their fronds from nearby. They must have been introduced. "Are we allowed to go there?" She was thinking of the colonies of sea birds or perhaps nesting turtles.

"Of course," he nodded. "I know these waters well. That's not a turtle breeding ground. There are two species. The green and the loggerhead. The birds will take off in clouds the moment we arrive but they soon settle back. Breeding activities are usually related to the amount of vegetation on the island, with particular species concentrating on particular cays. We're pretty near the mainland so these cays are home to sea and land birds. The sea birds play a big part in the cycling of plant nutrients from the sea to the islands. Those slender birds, circling overhead with the narrow wings and the pointed bills are terns."

"They have forked tails?" Eden commented, staring up.

"That's why a lot of people call them sea swallows. The noddies are the medium-sized birds. The ones with the dark plumage and the white heads. You can't miss the gulls. There are countless thousands of birds on the wooded cays and islands of the Reef. I'll have a word with Owen about visiting the cay. Robbie will enjoy it." He glanced away as he spoke, lifting a long arm to acknowledge Delma's wave.

"Looks like lunch is ready," he told Eden. He stood up, hand out, looking down at her. She was *so* beautiful. Her slender body was just covered in a high-cut one-piece swim-suit of purple Lycra with a diagonal trail of pink hibiscus. All the time they'd been lying there he'd wanted to seize her, to bury his face in her flowery fragrance spiked by the scent of the sea, to rain passionate kisses down on her. But he wasn't going to touch her. He was going to treat her like his favourite young cousin. He well knew that was going to be painfully difficult.

As he brought her to her feet, she looked into his eyes. Not a deliberate siren call but it might as well have been. It made his heart contract. It was more a plea mixed up with a little personal agony. *I want you,* even as she pulled back.

Woman, thy name is perversity!

Ah, well, he could wait, he thought, releasing her the instant she was upright. It wasn't every man who had such impressive self-control!

Lunch was delicious. Fresh crab with little home-baked rolls, ocean prawns, tiny lobsters, Queenslanders called "bugs", some really luscious home-grown avocados, a beautiful green salad and the best potato salad Eden thought she'd ever tasted—pesto in the mayonnaise—though it didn't appeal to Robbie who made his mother make him a basket of chips.

At first Delma declined a trip to the coral cay saying she'd seen it all before, but Robbie, as excited as if it were a trip to Treasure Island, insisted she come.

Lang rowed them over the crystal-clear waters, scorning the outboard. Eden watched his sleek muscles move beneath his dark golden skin unable to break her fascination. Nearing the shore she plunged into the sparkling, clear water, heart fluttering in delight, striking out towards the shore.

"Eden, Eden!" she heard Robbie call excitedly after her. She stopped, trod water watching him jump in feet first. She already knew he could swim. In fact Delma had told her proudly Robbie was the best swimmer in his class in a part of the world where children became proficient from age two. As the two approached the shore, just as Lang told her, their arrival put to flight clouds of sea birds that wheeled and dipped while emitting loud shrieks. Eden had never seen such a display, on the one hand not wishing to cause the birds alarm, but thrilled by the sight of them so abundant in the sky. Hand in hand she and Robbie set foot on the coral sand, which was pure white in the brilliant sunlight.

"Do you think we'll find treasure?" Robbie asked. "It could be over there in those silvery trees. Do you know what they're called?" he asked with an owlish air.

"No, I don't. I hope you can tell me." Eden shook back her long wet hair, revelling in the refreshing coolness of her body after its contact with the sea.

"Tawny forts. I think that's it," Robbie said, screwing up his eyes.

"Oh, I know." It suddenly came to her from her visits to the tourist islands. "Tournefortias. They make quite a contrast to those big strap leaves of the pandanus."

"With the orange pineapples?"

"Right." Eden turned her head as the others came ashore, not surprised that Delma made a beeline for her small son, her bare feet sinking into the sand.

"Don't ever do that again, Roberto," she cried, the words spraying out of her mouth with the wind. "You could have stood on something in the water."

"Like what?" Robbie demanded, looking very much like his father as his sunny mood changed.

"Like a piece of coral," his mother told him crossly.

"Not around here. There's no reef," Robbie pointed out intelligently, taking hold of Eden's hand.

"There could have been some coarse rubble," Delma insisted.

"He's right, Delma." Eden tried a soothing voice, when she really wanted to vent her irritation. "And he's a good swimmer." She smiled down on the child.

"Please don't try to go over my head, Eden." Delma crouched down to peer at Robbie's mutinous face. "I know what's best for my son."

"No you don't!" Robbie mumbled, already in revolt with his mother's possessiveness.

"Everything all right here?" Owen asked, coming slowly across the sand to them, while Lang dragged the boat up the strand.

"Everything's fine!" Eden told him calmly. "I can't wait to explore. Robbie thinks there might be treasure."

His father laughed. "There could be at that." Owen fully intended to leave a handful of coins tied into a handkerchief some place where his son could find it.

"Don't go too far away," Delma warned predictably, unsuctioning her frown.

"God, Delma, do you ever let up?" Owen flashed his wife an impatient glance. "There's nothing on this little cay that could possibly harm anyone. We've been on coral cays like this a million times."

Robbie waited for Lang to join them, then he yanked on Lang's hand. "Come on, Uncle Lang." He pointed to the silver-leaved trees. "Dad thinks there could be treasure."

"You lot go ahead." Owen took his wife's hand to move up the beach into the shade. "Delma and I are going to relax." He needed them to be gone in order to hide the little cache of glinting coins.

They had a fine time exploring the coral cay.

"One day we'll come back here alone," Lang promised her, his glance filled with pure desire.

"I'd like that." Vast areas of experience awaited her! She had never known a man who could make love with his eyes.

They walked together, hands and arms sometimes touching, an incredible intimacy, while Robbie ran a little way ahead. Lang pointed out all the things of interest while Eden looked about her with dazzled, love-struck eyes. Some of the trees had attained quite a height, soaring some seventy feet into the air. Once, looking up at their large pale green leaves, she had almost tripped over a buttress root only to have Lang haul her back. A few isolated moments crushed against his warm sea-sheened body. A kiss on her nape. Not brotherly at all. Moments that left her feeling her blood was full of burning stars.

Of course Robbie found his treasure, knowing perfectly well where it came from but keeping up the adventure. He fell into his father's lap shouting about his discovery. Delma smiled her pleasure, though it occurred to Eden her father and Delma had been having "a discussion." Taking time off at Marella Downs was starting to sound better by the moment.

It wasn't until they were almost ready to leave when Delma's ever-present fears actually materialised.

Eden and Robbie were standing in the shallows, Robbie playing some game of his own, when with a loud whoop he suddenly decided to race back to where his mother and father were sitting beneath the coconut palms. Lang was a distance off, looking over the dinghy. From nowhere, out of the cloudless blue sky, a large white bird with a frightening wingspan flew out of the trees gliding like a missile towards the running child all the while emitting raucous croaks.

"Robbie!" Eden cried frantically, her heart lurching. *"Stand still."* She swung her arms in a futile effort to divert the huge bird. Surely it couldn't mistake the running child for prey? She was close enough to see its large hooked beak and the powerful talons.

Robbie kept running, too frightened to stop. Eden gathered herself then launched herself across the sand, reaching the child with a dazzling burst of speed. She shielded him with her body bringing them both down onto the sand. She felt the bird move down over her. She could smell it. She could hear the continual flap of its wings. The nape of her neck hunched in revulsion and panic. It kept up its gut-shaking shrieks, the span of its wings throwing a large shadow on the sand.

She heard human voices, though she couldn't emit a single sound. Next she felt the bird's talon. *She* was now the focus of its rage. Please, God, don't let it hurt me! she prayed.

She felt the sharp sting, and then the pain.

Feathers were flying, grey and white. She could see strong brown legs. Lang's. Hear his harsh shout. Then he was lifting her up, holding her against his hip, while he got a hand to Robbie, who was lying pressed into the coral sand.

Owen and Delma had come running. Delma frantic with distress.

"God Almighty! I've never seen anything like that!" Owen burst out in horrified amazement, his face set with shock. "A sea eagle. A rogue. I think you've knocked it out, Lang. Maybe killed it."

Lang didn't respond. He was blaming himself. He wondered how he could possibly have missed the sea eagle's nest. Usually they were in the fork of trees. Or maybe the nest was on the ground. Either way in the breeding season the nests became too large to miss. This wasn't the breeding season yet this bird had *attacked*. There was no other word for it. Eden had a long bleeding scratch on her back, that followed the shape of the bird's talon. He didn't have to point it out. Everyone looked at her in utter dismay.

"My dear, you're bleeding!" Delma studied the red tracks, her face expressing her very real concern. "That was so brave of you. Thank you. Thank you." She pressed her small dazed son to her.

Owen agreed feelingly, smoothing his daughter's arm. "Are you all right, sweetheart? How horrible for that to happen. I'm so sorry. But it's quite extraordinary, you know. We're talking sea eagles not nesting magpies."

"Let's wash this off in the sea," Lang said, acutely aware of Eden's shock. He lifted her in his arms like she was a featherweight, walking down the strand, not stopping until they reached the water, where he moved out a way so he could submerge Eden's whole body. He lowered himself with her, keeping his arms around her in case she suffered some reaction.

"Okay?" He was fairly shocked himself, sick at the whole

incident. Perhaps he'd have to destroy the bird. He had swiped at it hard enough but incredibly it wouldn't give way.

She was muttering to herself quietly, still stunned by the bird's attack. "I'll be all right in a minute or so. What was that anyway? It was like something out of Hitchcock?"

He stared intently at her pale face, alert for any sudden faint spell though she seemed to be characteristically in possession of herself.

"It looked a bit like it," he answered wryly. "I've seen quite a few bird attacks over the years, mostly nesting plovers. Nothing like what I witnessed today. It shouldn't have happened. The whole thing was bizarre."

"Absolutely." She ducked her head momentarily beneath the water, feeling not a whole lot more stable. All around them, the sea, aquamarine in the shallows glittered and the spice-scented breeze blew from the cay.

"The salt water should help a lot," Lang told her soothingly. "I'll send a message ahead to have a doctor waiting at the house."

"You don't think I need a doctor?" Eden looked over her shoulder in dismay. "I mean does it need stitching?"

He kept his eyes on her back. As the water washed the blood away it welled again, but to his great relief not badly. "I don't think so. There's a first-aid kit aboard but we'll let a doctor take a look at it. I'd hate to see that beautiful skin damaged."

"I'll survive." She gave him a shadow of her smile. "And thank you for my rescue."

"Take it as part of my devotion," he said, with a return to the sardonic. "If you feel a little better, I'd like to get you back to the boat. You can lie down. So can Robbie. He got quite a fright, poor little fellow."

"He'll soon turn it into an adventure," Eden said thankfully. "No need to fuss over me." When actually she was looking forward to lying down, having him continue to look at her with such concern in his silvery-grey eyes.

And now it was Lang who knew beyond any whisper of doubt. He wanted to fuss over this beautiful creature for the rest of her life.

CHAPTER NINE

EDEN was already three days into her stay on Marella Downs, the Forsyth stronghold since the mid-1800s. She had been welcomed with open arms, her rapport with Lang's family instant and mutual. West of the Great Dividing Range she quickly found was another world. An infinite *vastness* of sweeping sun-burnt plains, of *brownness,* stretching thousands of kilometres away to the Great Sandy Desert. The grasses of the savannahs where the great herd grazed were bleached to a uniform dark gold. The sun beat down from a cloudless peacock-blue sky. This was the Outback, as different to the tropical coastal strip with its lush panoramas as the far side of the moon.

Lang had flown them in the company plane, a Beechcraft King Air. It was a smooth flight without incident, but once over the rugged grape-blue ranges with their jagged ridges, deep chasms and gorges, the landscape had changed dramatically. From the voluptuous green of the watershed East to a *dry, dry* land. It was vast and empty. To Eden's uninitiated eyes, *daunting.* She suspected it would be brutally hot, but when they landed to the family welcoming party she found the heat was quite without the high humidity of the seaboard. In a way, more comfortable. Tomorrow they were to make the return journey. She to her father's house. Her relationship with Delma had thawed considerably since the incident with the sea eagle, certainly the just beneath the surface antipathy had diminished, but Eden knew they would never be exactly simpatico. Delma couldn't let go of the power. Just another fact of life!

Lang's mother, on the other hand, was a lovely warm, tolerant woman with a humorous personality. Barbara Forsyth made a deep impression on her. Eden found to her delighted surprise she could share things with Barbara; viewpoints affecting family that she had never been able to express with anyone else. That included her own mother who had switched off very early in life. Barbara was different. She had known great happiness and great despair, suffered many painful lessons, but she had survived it all in the process learning how to make loving contact with the people around her. Georgia, Lang's sister, shared her mother's warm embracing nature. The friendship they so readily offered affected Eden deeply. Quite simply it gladdened her sore heart.

True to his word, Lang made sure they did things together, riding out early morning and late afternoon, or taking the jeep, visiting the natural features that were abundant on the station. Their fascination made her change her superficial judgment of the harsh environment. Its beauty had nothing to do with the flamboyant beauty of the tropics and its dense orchid-bearing rainforests. This was a beauty that like a difficult, powerful painting needed study. The sheer *size,* the open spaces and the empty natural landscape were the overwhelming factors. Then there was the gorgeous ever-present bird life, there were literally explosions of birds out of the trees whenever one passed. There were snakes, of course, huge goannas and legions of kangaroos and wallabies made a marvellous sight in numbers bounding across the grasslands. This was powerful, primitive, country with large tracts of wilderness. In the billabongs and rivers, only a little further north, *crocodile* were plentiful.

The last day Lang planned to take her to the "best Marella has to offer."

"He's been keeping it for last," Georgia told her. "You'll be absolutely captivated." They were lingering over breakfast.

"Do I get to hear what it is?" she asked with a smile.

"That's a surprise." Lang turned to request more coffee from Grace, their part-aboriginal housekeeper. Grace had

been born on the station and never wished to leave it. Like
the Forsyth women, she doted on Lang.

The first thing Eden remarked on meeting the family was
the fact Barbara and Georgia were *blond* with clear green
eyes; their tall, athletic bodies in tip-top condition. Both did
many outdoor chores around the station while Georgia's husband, Brad, an attractive six-footer, also fairish in colouring,
handled the management. An arrangement that worked very
well. Ryan, their little son, who was spending part of his
holiday with Brad's parents was also blond in colouring she
was told. Lang with his raven hair, olive skin and silver eyes
was the changeling until she saw the portrait of his grandfather, Zachary.

As she was the image of her mother, Lang was the image
of his paternal grandfather. She marvelled at the power of
genetics!

Eden was in her very comfortable guest room changing
from the cotton dress she had worn at breakfast to more
workmanlike gear, or as workmanlike as she could manage,
a long-sleeved cotton shirt to protect her arms and cotton
jeans, both midnight-blue in colour, when Barbara came to
the door.

"Eden, dear, I have to tell you we have an unexpected
visitor," she said gently but in such a way Eden responded.

"You don't sound too happy about it?" She stood aside
so Barbara could enter the room.

"Well I can't say it comes as a complete surprise,"
Barbara sighed. "Lara has a penchant for popping in when
Lang's about."

"*That* Lara?" Eden knew a moment of absolute dismay.
This holiday had been perfect so far.

"*That* Lara." Barbara raised a hand to her brow. "It's only
a flying visit."

"Does she know I'm here?"

"What do *you* think?" Barbara asked, a trace acerbically,
looking at Eden with her clear green eyes.

"Delma must have told her. They're very close."

"Well...no worries." Barbara shrugged to overcome her mild exasperation. "Georgia has her jobs to do but I can entertain Lara while you and Lang see the canyon. Darn," she broke off in self-annoyance, "I've given it away."

Eden's voice filled with amusement. "That's okay. I won't tell. I'm sure Lara will want to come along."

"Look, it's *your* holiday," Barbara pointed out. "I'm certain you don't want her to go."

"No." Their minds were finely in tune.

"Then you'd better hurry up. Lara can get in where the ants can't."

"I'm ready!" Eden made such a dash into the dressing room to collect her white akubra Barbara burst out laughing.

"I'll tell Lara you'll both be back for lunch. I don't like to be rude..."

"As if you could be," Eden scoffed.

They found Lara sitting in what the family called "the old drawing room." She was regarding a magnificent landscape painting rather grimly.

"So sorry, Lara." Barbara excused her temporary absence with a smile. "Here's Eden." Somehow it came out like a masterstroke.

"How are you, Lara?" Eden spoke brightly, moving further into the room. "I didn't expect to see you," she said without emphasis, wanting to load her voice with sarcasm but characteristically not doing so.

"I just flew over to say hello," Lara told her, finishing her head to toe inspection of Eden's slender figure.

"Lang was here. What happened to him?" Barbara asked.

"He's outside having a word with Brad," Lara told her. "Are you enjoying yourself, Eden?" Lara swivelled her head from the open French doors leading to the front veranda back to Eden.

"I've had a lovely time." Eden touched Barbara's arm softly, her face filled with affection. "Barbara and the family have made me feel so much at home."

"But then you've never really had a home, have you?" Lara asked, sounding warmly sympathetic.

"I don't know how you can say that, Lara?" Barbara intervened rather crisply. "It's certainly not true."

"You *do* know what I mean?" Lara's voice turned apologetic. "Delma told me the whole story. It couldn't have been easy for you, Eden."

"I didn't know Delma knew the whole story." Eden was unimpressed by Lara's contrition. "I certainly never told her. Anyway we won't speak of it. I'm so looking forward to today."

"Where are you going?" Lara asked, not trying to disguise her avid curiosity.

"I'm not exactly sure. It's a surprise."

"I love surprises! I'm sure you can fit me in. I started to tell Lang I'd love to go riding. It seems so long since we've done it. Ah, speak of the man! Here he is!" Lara's face lit as if touched with a ray of sunshine.

Lang strode into the room looking marvellous in an open-necked bush shirt and jeans. He levelled them all with his quick penetrating glance. "Time to be off, Eden," he said briskly, "if we're to be back for lunch. I hope you'll be staying until then, Lara?"

Lara, seated firmly in the chair looked like she could outlast any of them. "Actually I was hoping to come with you and Eden," she said in a brittle voice.

"That'd be nice, but you wouldn't want to see it again," Lang assured her, getting a grip on Eden's arm. "Barbara is on her own. I'm sure she'd love some company."

It was possible a tear came to Lara's eyes. "So where are you going?" she demanded. "Tell me the truth."

"The truth is the best way," Lang informed her with a quirk of a smile. "But this time it's a secret."

"It can't be!" Lara insisted.

"Life is full of frustrating things."

"It sounds like something I might enjoy." Lara revealed the full extent of her disappointment.

"Actually Lara it's Eden's *first* time," Barbara murmured tactfully. "She'll form the best impressions if Lang takes her on her own."

"It can't be the caves." Lara came swiftly to her feet, an attractive figure in a black-and-white silk shirt and white hipsters.

"Not the caves," Lang agreed smoothly, silver eyes travelling to his mother's. "I told Brad to let Georgia know Lara has arrived. She'll want to come back to the house. You girls can have morning tea. Catch up on all the news."

"Thank you, darling," Barbara said sweetly, with a smoothness of her own. "Enjoy yourselves."

Lang sketched a brief salute. "We'll be back for lunch. Make it for one—one-thirty."

"Yes, dear," said Barbara, and snapped her fingers.

"I think it'd be fair to say that was cruel," Eden remarked as they drove out of the home compound.

"Would you have preferred I invited her?" Lang gave her an ironic look.

Eden sighed. "She made me feel sad. I don't know why. She thinks she's in love with you."

"I'd rather hear *you'd* fallen in love with me," he said.

It was the first time in quite a while she'd heard even a flash of his seductive voice. In fact Lang had kept strictly to his promise of "backing off." The only trouble Eden found was she couldn't be in his presence half a minute without "turning on."

"Now we've gone and left her with Barbara," she said, totally evading his question.

"Don't worry. My mother handles these situations extremely well," he said with amusement.

"What situations?" She turned her head to stare at his handsome chiselled profile. "Ex-girlfriends turning up?"

"Would you like to hear something?" He gave a brief laugh. "It happens all the time."

"So many of them."

"None of them as defenceless as you," he told her. "Lara was a girlfriend for a while. I didn't love her. I didn't ask her to marry me."

"But you slept with her?"

"What do you want me to say? We had crazy times together?"

"I can believe it," she said in heartfelt tones.

"Not until I met *you*."

Her heart contracted. "Big brother," she reminded him.

"I think I've taken extremely good care of you." He nodded. "In fact we'd become almost family."

"I love your family." She looked out the window at the flying miles.

"They think you're special, as well."

"I've really never spoken so much in depth with another woman until I met your mother," she confided. "Not my girlfriends, and I have good, long-standing friends. Not my own mother. I was so protective of her. I used to think she was so sensitive if I said the wrong thing to her it would leave an actual bruise on her white skin." A pause. "She didn't have to live the life she did."

He took in her poignant expression. "I'm really sorry, Eden. I wish I'd known you when you were a little girl. Sometimes I see flashes of you when you were very young. Small, soft, so very, very, vulnerable."

"The holiday will be over tomorrow."

"Don't sound like that," he said, briskly. "You can come again anytime you like."

"I should go home," she answered, very seriously. "My grandfather may need me."

"Your grandfather made his life," Lang found himself answering very seriously. "By the same token it occurs to me some healing might be effected if he and Owen made their peace."

Eden stared at him, her whole attention captured. "What an extraordinary idea!"

"Is it?" He faintly shrugged. "Your grandfather must

be feeling utterly guilty and down. He thought he was doing the right thing at the time. That was his way. But they all suffered because of his decision. Your mother, your father, the man who reared you, your grandfather. Most of all, *you*, the innocent victim.''

"Dad hates my grandfather," Eden said quietly. "He blames him for bringing so much unhappiness to his and my mother's life."

"But that's not really true, is it?" Lang threw her a glance. "I can't see you marrying a man you didn't love. Pregnant or not. Though times have changed."

"Well, of course they have. We're all different. Not everyone is as sunny and loving towards people as your mother for example."

"True. But my mother emerged from her own terrible depression after my father died. It was a very painful experience but she came out of it with such strength. I'm very proud of my mother. And my sister."

"As they are of you. I didn't have that sort of family."

"But you will have," he said, momentarily reaching out to her. "You'll marry. Have children of your own."

"I hope so."

"In fact you should be thinking of getting married right now," he told her, sardonic eyes seeking hers. "I see twenty-four as a good age for a woman."

"And thirty-two for a man? You've certainly sown your wild oats."

"Nonsense!" he scoffed. "I was never 'wild' as you phrase it. I was too busy re-making my family's life."

The surprise, located about ten miles from the homestead, turned out to be a corridor of grandly sculptured creamy yellow cliffs. In many places, Eden saw the sandstone walls had been rendered smooth as butter she supposed by millions of years of weathering. Tall white-boled gums lined the cliff tops for the full length of the canyon with groves of magnificent palms and tree ferns. A permanent shallow creek glittered and snaked down the centre maybe thirty feet wide but

Lang informed her after heavy monsoonal rains flash floods could turn its placid meandering into a raging torrent.

Silently they made their way through the entrance into the naturally created amphitheatre. Eden staring around her with wonder. Another Outback phenomenon! Lush havens in the middle of a rugged, extremely dry terrain. River she-oaks grew along the creek, many coloured bottlebrushes, and quite unexpectedly stands of flowering wild hibiscus, here pink, there yellow with other shrubs covered in red flowers much like frangipani. With the canyon shaded by its high walls for much of the day numerous delicate plants were able to thrive. Ferns, mosses, orchids, native violets, and beautiful little wildflowers with faces of great charm. Great boulders, too, littered the canyon floor, some of fantastic shape. Some standing vertically, as tall as Lang. It was very still as they picked their way around them, the temperature much cooler in the canyon than the heat of the savannah. Eden found the idea of splashing her face and hands in the clear fresh stream irresistible. It didn't matter if in doing so she wet her trainers and the hem of her cotton jeans. They would soon dry off in the hot sun.

"That was so refreshing!" She came back to Lang, turning up a joyous face to the sun. "This is a fantastic place," she laughed, holding her damp shirt from her breasts. "Thank you for bringing me here."

"I'm glad you're enjoying it." His voice mocked and indulged her. "However, here's your hat." He had been holding it now he handed it back to her with a snap.

She shoved the akubra back on her head not caring that with her hair tied in a thick plait she looked little more than a schoolgirl. "With you around I never get to remove it." It was said with the greatest good humour and the touching innocence of a girl.

He didn't much care for it now when he was spending his time coping with insistent sexual pressure. He watched her move ahead, with delicate grace, her footing light and sure. Here and there she touched a hand to some of the smooth boulders, turning to exclaim to him in surprise when she found the seemingly smooth surface surprisingly rough in texture.

"The boulders contain feldspar, quartz, other minerals, that's why," he called in his role of Big Brother.

When the rocky gaps became a little difficult to negotiate, she hesitated. "You'll have to give me a hand, Lang. Or shouldn't we take this route? Some of these boulders seem to be balanced rather precariously?" She looked up. They were, in fact, one on top of the other.

"Just hang on there," he warned her immediately, quickening his pace. He'd been deriving so much pleasure from just looking at her exploring he had deliberately hung back. It was another way of handling his ever-present urge to make love to her. That wasn't going to happen until she was ripe for it. This visit, though miraculously harmonious in some ways had been very hard on him. He was a fiercely passionate man who couldn't display it. Playing Big Brother to this particular young woman was excruciating. Once he had his hands on her; around her narrow waist, he couldn't seem to take them away. It was harder than anything he had ever done though he knew by now he had never even approached this level of feeling.

But she astonished him. Standing on the rock above him, she leaned over him, beautiful violet eyes fixed on his face, her hands slipping along his shoulders. "I don't understand a damn thing about myself," she confessed solemnly. "I've loved being here with you, yet in some ways it's been a penance."

He could empathize with that right through to his bones. "Yes," he answered harshly, before he completely lost it. "Don't start anything you can't stop. Aren't you the girl who told me she wasn't ready to join the grown-ups?"

To Eden, after their remarkable affinity of the morning, it seemed like a total breath-taking rebuff. "All right, I understand." She straightened up immediately, experiencing deep painful flickers of humiliations. "Has it got something to do with Lara's turning up?"

Desire surged then burned its way through him. He welcomed it even as it consumed him with an odd sexual hostility. "You don't understand a damn thing."

For an instant more she stood motionless, incredibly still, then she said, very softly, "Go to hell!"

Before he could stop her, she stepped straight off the boulder onto the next one, apparently in a great hurry to get away from him and wasn't going to pretend otherwise.

"Eden!" his voice cracked out urgently, the sharpness of his tone echoing down the empty canyon. The scratches on her back from the sea eagle attack hadn't even faded almost a fortnight later yet now she was risking possible injury to her ankle. God, she pressed him hard, inciting every known emotion in him.

Within a few feet she lost her footing, just as he feared, slipping down a high boulder, feet scrabbling for purchase before she hit the sand. He felt the shuddering vibration as though it had hit his own spine. "Damn it, Eden!" He moved easily over the rocks from long experience, jumping the last few feet. "Don't you know how to play it safe?"

"I guess not." She was careful not to get up. Not for a minute or two, though she was certain she had done no more than jar her body. Serve her right!

He was almost tempted to slap her, fingers itching. Anything to make contact. Instead he crouched down, staring at her. "It's a wonder you've got breath left in your body. How's your back? There's grit all over your shirt." He brushed at it. "As if those scratches weren't enough."

"Want to heal me?" The words burst from her mouth. Not provocatively but practically a plea.

"I can take a look." No matter how badly he wanted it, if he began to make love to her he knew he wouldn't stop. He rolled her very gently, loosening her shirt from her jeans, hitching it up. He could smell the special fragrance that came

off her skin, like a field of wildflowers mixed with the heat
off her body. Clean, womanly, intensely attractive.

She lay perfectly still, skin quivering, her breath ragged,
heart drumming into the sand. He hadn't touched her yet she
thought she might pass out from an excess of sensation. And
then he did, his touch exquisitely gentle, but leaving a trail
of fire....

The long scratches to one side of her back had healed quickly
and well. Soon they would be invisible, yet the sight of them
on her beautiful skin upset him. Her shirt had greatly diminished grazing but she winched slightly when he touched a
reddened area.

"Okay?"

"I'm fine," she said stoically, knowing her fit of bravado
could have ended in worse injury.

"You can take a deep breath?"

"Sure I can."

He pulled down her shirt, let it hang loose. "So all's well
that ends well!"

She sat up, not looking at him. Her hat had come off during her wild slide. She didn't know where it had landed.
Didn't care. One glance into his silver eyes and she'd be in
over her head, much like the peaceful shallow creek that ran
in front of her could turn into a torrent.

He helped her regain her footing, though he noticed she
was very careful not to cling to him, staring sightlessly at the
glinting sand.

Only he couldn't stand it any longer.

"Come here." He pulled her in to him, holding her tightly
to his body. The knowledge that he could do no more than
kiss her only deepened the painful ache of desire. "You
know how much I want you?"

"Yes." Her voice was little more than a whisper.

"We're quite alone. No one will come. I could take you
easily only I can't let you down. I don't want you waking
up one morning to find yourself pregnant. I don't want you

experiencing any fears, Eden.'' He felt her tremble, misin-
terpreted it. ''I'm not going to seduce you.''

It was her chance to say she desperately wanted him to;
that it was an okay time for her, only some semblance of
sense remained. Soon they would have to go back to the
homestead. She knew if they made love she couldn't possibly
hide that fact from anyone. Everything about her would
scream the message. Echoes to follow. Wave after wave of
them.

He let a kiss trail down over her face, his hard passion
deliberately channelled towards tender and protective, until
he reached her mouth. It was pure ecstasy. With his hands
he found her beautiful breasts, his fingers slipping buttons
so he could caress them more intimately. She let him. Not
staying him for a moment.

I want to be inside her, he thought recklessly. I want to
finish what I start. I want to adore her. She had to cling to
him while he muttered, ''Oh God, Oh God,'' over and over
into her ear. How did one define love? he thought in some
torment. Seizing the moment no matter what? Or caring for
what came after? He was hyper-aware of the effect her
mother's sad life had had on her. He used to have wonderful
control. Surely to God it wasn't shot to hell?

''We can't continue like this,'' he warned her, even as his
mouth burnished the skin of her neck. It was the truth. But
how to act on it? It was difficult when she wasn't helping
him, responding to his every touch as though it lifted her to
heaven.

Help came like something out of a storybook. At first he
couldn't believe it. As he stood with Eden's dark curly head
tucked beneath his chin he sensed rather than saw movement
at the canyon's entrance. His eyes narrowed, body tensing.
There were dingoes in the area. He had seen giant goannas
before today. Before long he saw what had caused it, amazed
at how fanciful it seemed. The greatest, most extravagantly
beautiful surprise. Like an omen. He spoke barely above a
whisper so as not to startle Eden or the graceful intruder that

moved into his line of vision. "Don't move. Look towards the entrance."

Eden lifted her head slowly, arrested by a note approaching awe in Lang's vibrant voice. Even alerted, she couldn't control her gasp of absolute delight. Knife-keen pleasure shot through her. An exceptionally beautiful, pure white horse was wandering down the canyon, most probably seeking water. Mane and tail turned to platinum as the sunlight poured down on it. Eden had seen nothing like this before. She drank in the sight as though this vision like some mythical unicorn had been sent especially to help her through an enormously fraught time. The horse, which was light and smallish, put her in mind of the Spanish-bred Andalusian. It turned right on, ears pricking. Not nervous, excited though, it had scented them already. There was little breeze in the canyon to carry their scent away from it. Yet the horse seemed to accept their presence. It walked on to the water, bowing its delicate head to the stream.

They stood perfectly still while it drank. Eden, her face radiant, now leaning back against Lang, his arms enfolding her. "This is the loveliest thing I've seen in my life." Eden's violet eyes glowed. "Where did it come from?"

"I'd be fascinated to know," Lang murmured into her hair. "Brad hasn't mentioned it. It's a brumby. Dished head, Arab blood, but the prettiest little brumby I've ever seen."

"And pure white." Eden was enormously surprised. "All it needs is a single straight horn with a spiral twist."

"And eyes as blue as yours."

"How I'd love to ride it!" The lift-off! For all she knew it might sprout wings.

"How I'd love to see you on it. But it might just be a mirage." He laughed a little at the thought. The white horse, having drunk its fill, was already making its way out of the canyon, picking its way delicately, without hurry. Finally it disappeared through the natural arch.

"Is it me or did time stand still?" Eden asked with shining eyes.

He could feel the life force in her body.

"Have you ever thought passion is a kind of miracle?" He bent over her, exultant as she lifted her face for his kiss.

"I know I'm going to remember this all my life," Eden responded with fervour.

CHAPTER TEN

WHEN Robbie heard the story of the mysterious white horse—for no one on Marella station had yet sighted it—he was captivated. This in turn led to a spiralling enthusiasm to have a pony of his own. "More than anything I want to learn to ride," he told Eden with a shining look in his eyes. Christmas was less than a week away; the ideal time to receive a wonderful present. He was six, going on seven. Eden had told him all about her early adventures on horseback. A pony was the best thing in the world! Now nothing would suit but she should see to it right away. He made Eden promise she would speak to their father about it first thing in the morning.

"He'll listen to you," said Robbie, remarkably shrewd for his age.

These days Delma was rarely at home, caught up by a non-stop flurry of pre-Christmas functions, but when she was there, she began a campaign of conveying to Eden by way of smiling remarks Eden might want to start thinking of a place of her own. Preferably in the New Year. As if Eden hadn't thought of just that many times herself. In this house, huge by any standards, Delma made Eden feel two adult women couldn't possibly reside under the one roof. Certainly not Cassandra's daughter. The remarks were always timed for when Owen and the highly perceptive Robbie weren't around, which came as no surprise. As Eden had expected, Delma knew all about Lara's visit to Marella and Lang's "surprisingly cavalier treatment of her."

"Really it was like a slap in the face, Lara told me. It upset her dreadfully. I know Lang can be very unco-operative from time to time, but he and Lara are so close. You didn't

have a word with him, did you?'' Delma's expression con-
veyed the reason might well have been selfish, pea-brained
behaviour on Eden's part.

Christmas week, but where was the goodwill?

They were finishing brunch on that Saturday morning when
Eden brought up the subject of a pony for Robbie. Robbie
had been nudging her surreptitiously right through the leisurely meal but she had waited until the optimum moment.

''I'd be happy to give him lessons,'' she concluded, ''if
that helps.''

Robbie beamed at her. Big sister, Eden, solving all his
problems.

Delma, however, had concerns. ''That's a kind offer, Eden,
but Roberto is only six years old.''

''Nearly seven.'' Robbie gulped. He hated it when his
mother flatly opposed his plans. ''Eden could ride a horse
before she could walk,'' he said.

Delma laughed. ''Clever thing! But we couldn't keep a
horse here. It would be a waste of money.''

''Now when did that ever bother you?'' Owen, who had
been enjoying the beautiful morning with his family, suddenly threw down his linen napkin. ''Think you could hold
off until your birthday, Robbie?'' he addressed his son.

Robbie didn't hesitate. ''Of course. You're serious, Dad?''
His dark eyes grew huge.

''Probably I should have thought of it myself,'' Owen considered. ''It seems extraordinary but it had to be forcibly
brought home to me I'm a dad.''

''Well thanks for that!'' Delma burst out. ''Robbie is your
only son. Your heir. Not Eden. You chose to ignore her for
over twenty years.''

Owen looked down the table at his wife. He knew he had
been putting off this particular piece of information too long.
Now it was time to get it out. ''Actually, my dear, I'm glad
we're all together. We can get this thing straightened out.
I've had Blake Howard draw up a new will.''

Delma sat back shocked, staring at her husband, alarm in her eyes.

"Naturally there are changes," Owen said. "If you settle down, Delma, you might hear."

Instantly the atmosphere in the luxurious informal dining room degenerated like a bad weather report coming up.

Here it comes, Eden thought with a sinking heart. She understood Delma's banked-up fury. She'd told her father clearly it would be better if he left her out of his will entirely. Her mother had left her an annual income by way of a trust. Not a great amount of money but it would take care of all the extra. There were also the proceeds from the sale of the house in Brisbane. The important thing was she was a trained lawyer. Her job in the firm her great-grandfather had founded was there for her when she wanted it.

Owen was speaking but Eden barely heard him. Robbie, who always liked to sit beside her, had even stopped feeding the family cat, Baba, under the table. He took hold of Eden's hand, eyeing off his taut-faced mother uncertainly.

"You can't mean this, Owen," Delma protested bleakly.

"I do mean it, Delma." Owen clenched his determined jaw.

"I won't accept it." Delma stabbed at her hair.

"Tough. It's done. Though why you're looking so utterly deprived I'll never know."

Delma glared at him. "Roberto is your heir. Boys are important. Eden will marry within a year or so. She's trying hard enough to land Lang!" The words hung in the air like black clouds.

Robbie raised his head to his sister, baffled. "What's land Lang mean?" he whispered, thinking it might have something to do with fishing.

Eden inched closer, lowering her voice. "I don't always follow the way your mother talks, either, Robbie."

Robbie nodded, as though that made good sense.

"You know very well what I mean." Delma heaved herself to her feet, a glamorous figure, with her hair, make-up and dress, perfect even at ten o'clock on a lazy Saturday morning. "I have it on good authority that's exactly what you're doing."

It couldn't have been Lara. Shock. Horror.

"Sit down, Delma," Owen ordered wearily. "I hate to say this but you're getting very tiresome. No doubt your girl-friend, Lara, is helping you out. No way is Eden trying to land Lang as you so sweetly put it. I'm wondering if they didn't fall madly in love with each other on sight. None of which concerns you. If anything happens to me you'll be left a rich woman. Robbie will have a tidy fortune to set him up. I have my charities to look after. Certain bequests. There's absolutely no way I'm going to leave Robbie so rich he'll start thinking he doesn't have to do much with his life. I'm convinced too much money too early can ruin a young man."

Delma sat down again, breathing so heavily she might have been in a marathon. "But you're going to leave it all to Eden?" she challenged.

"Dad..." Eden tried to intervene, but he waved her down.

"If I appear to have favoured you over Robbie, Eden, I haven't really. With you I have so much to make up for."

"What about *me*?" Delma demanded, like she would soon be on the street.

"Good God, Delma!" Owen burst out disgustedly. "I thought you were doing pretty well. If I've found out one damn thing, you married me for my money."

That rocked her. She sat back. "I didn't. I love you," she protested, holding one hand to her breast.

"That's hard to believe!" Owen's fine dark eyes flashed. "Try telling some of your friends you've been badly done by in my will. They'll be screeching with laughter behind your back. Something else you might remember. I'm still in my forties. I have no intention of dying for a very long while."

That did it for Robbie, who hadn't expected his mother's tirade. When he then heard talk of his father's "dying" he burst into tears, small shoulders heaving.

"Now see what you've done." Delma leapt up, lioness to her cub. She went to her son who fiercely resisted her.

"Listen, Robbie," Eden said urgently, getting a hold of Robbie's flailing arm. "Dad was trying to say he'll *always* be here for us. He's going to live to be one hundred."

"If it's not too much of a drag." Owen smiled ironically. "Come here, Robbie."

Instantly Robbie quietened. He pulled himself up, going to his father, who pushed back his chair so he could draw his son onto his knee.

"I love you, kiddo. Never forget it." Owen hugged him hungrily. "You're my boy. Heck you even look like me."

This was what Robbie was hungry for, Eden thought, looking on with satisfaction. Kisses and cuddles from his dad, wonderful moments together. The firm conviction he was important to his father.

"I love you, too, Dad," Robbie groaned with contentment as his father pulled him closer. "Please say I can have a pony."

"I thought we had that all sewn up." Owen ruffled his son's curls, restored to a good mood. "When you wake up on the morning of your seventh birthday a pony will be chewing the grass outside your window. Waiting for you to ride it."

"Wow!" The little boy was ecstatic.

"Forget about me." Delma, who was still standing, jammed Robbie's vacated chair into the table with a crash. "I'm nothing." Her cheeks were on fire with rage and humiliation. "Only the wife and mother."

For a split second Owen looked like he was thinking about reviewing that situation. "And a wonderful wife and mother you've been."

Alas it came out like sarcasm when that wasn't at all what Owen intended.

Delma turned on her heel, sailing from the room like a dispossessed queen, the high heels of her expensive sandals tapping out a fierce rhythm.

"Go to her, Dad," Eden pleaded. "All this talk of a will has upset her."

But Owen sat back in his chair, hugging Robbie to him. "Upset her be damned. It's about time my wife started to show a little heart, let alone sense."

When Owen didn't follow her up as he usually did, Delma worked herself into a fine rage using Eden as the scapegoat. Finally she thought to ring Lang. She had long looked to him for support. And he was a businessman! What Owen had done was cruel and unusual. Why he hadn't even discussed changing his will with her. Delma went to the door of the main bedroom she shared with her husband and locked herself in. Lang would share her legitimate concerns no matter his attraction to Eden. Women like that could steal any man's heart. Even one tough, self-contained character like Lang.

Mercifully, Lang answered, although he said at the outset he had agreed to a game of golf with his friend Bruno in a half hour's time.

Delma began hastily, launching into her woes as she saw them. Did Lang know Owen had changed his will? Did he know how unfairly she and Roberto had been treated? Did he realise behind Eden's lovely, innocent face, there was a clever, conniving mind? It was Eden without a doubt who was manipulating her father. It was Eden who pushed her father into changing his will, which gave her by far the lion's share. Delma spoke like a woman in dire financial need.

Lang listened mostly in a despairing silence thinking Delma couldn't see past her nose. Finally he told her he just couldn't buy any of it. Delma had convinced herself Eden was the enemy since Eden had entered their lives. He knew because Eden had told him she was already financially secure. He had seen plenty of evidence of it. He told Delma she shouldn't listen to Lara's gossip if she wanted to keep *their* friendship intact. For once he didn't mince words, convinced straight talking was the only answer. Delma as a matter of urgency had to re-think her position.

But Eden had to get out of there, he thought worriedly.
They had a crisis situation. And it was Christmas. He would
have to send Delma a card to remind her. On top of that,
they were all supposed to be attending a pre-Christmas party
that night. He would have to talk seriously to Eden. She had
changed all their lives in a way no one had planned.

Despite their spectacular fight, Owen and Delma, veteran ac-
tors, kept to their plan to attend the big pre-Christmas party
given by their friends, the Clark-Ryans. To have missed it
would have been unthinkable. Both of them had survived
countless arguments, afterwards putting on their masks.
Although her heart wasn't in a party mood, Eden desperately
wanted to see Lang. They'd talked most days on the phone
but this time of year was as function-packed for Lang as it
was for her father. A combination of business and pleasure.
She knew from her visit to Marella, Lang always spent
Christmas with his family. Which was just as it should be.
Tomorrow she would have to tell her father she planned to
spend the week from Christmas Eve to the New Year with
her grandfather with whom she kept in touch. Despite the
fact her grandfather assured her she didn't have to worry her
head about him, he had sounded touchingly grateful she
wanted to be with him.

So it was arranged. She knew Owen would be greatly upset and disappointed by her decision. Perhaps Robbie, too,
not that she didn't have lots of presents for him. He was such
an affectionate little boy but she knew in her heart it was the
right thing to do. Her grandfather needed her at that melan-
choly time; so wonderfully festive for others. At least Delma
would be relieved. Her father and Delma never settled for a
quiet family Christmas. As far as she could make out they
were having lots of friends and their children over to share
Christmas Day with them. Delma would be sure to arrange
a marvellous feast.

Only this wasn't the year for feasting, Eden thought, beset
by her own sad memories. This time last year she had her

mother with her. Maybe next year she would feel a little
better. Who knows! Where would she be then? It was a kind
of terror to contemplate the thought Lang mightn't be in her
life. Neither of them could deny the awesome power of passion but there were too many shifts and changes in life. Her
mother had experienced a grand passion but she hadn't lived
happily ever after. Maybe that only happened in short phases
of life.

When Lang arrived at the house he was told by the housekeeper, Mr. and Mrs. Carter had already left. Robbie was
tucked into bed. Eden he found waiting in the living room,
sable mane flowing, skin luminous against a very chic little
sequined dress hanging from tiny straps. It was a colour he
had never seen her in before. A soft but breath-taking poppy-
red. Colour-matched evening sandals were on her feet.
Around her neck she wore his sapphires, her father's gift of
sapphire and diamond earrings, both creating quite a dazzle.
The deep blue of the stones in no way clashed with her dress
but acted as a wonderful foil for her eyes.

She was smiling, hands outstretched, but he knew her too
well not to realise there was sadness at her heart. For that
matter he wasn't in the mood for a party, either. He just
wanted the two of them together. Quietly. Delma's phone
call had upset him. He could just imagine what effect
Delma's habitual histrionics was having on Eden. Strangely
with Owen they were like water off a duck's back.

"You look beautiful." He bent to kiss her cheek. "I've
never seen you in red. It suits you."

"It's Christmas. Delma was in very glamorous green.
You've just missed them."

"So Maria told me. We'd better get going. Unless I'm
very much mistaken we could have a storm before the night's
over. We're due for one."

"That might put a dampener on the party?"

"Don't worry. In the tropics we have these sorts of even-
tualities covered."

They'd pulled out of the driveway before Lang spoke. "You seem a little down?" He glanced at her profile.

The understatement of the year. She gave a little shrug. "I suppose I am." She glanced out the window, seeing the storm clouds sail across the moon. "Dad stirred everything up by saying he'd changed his will."

"Oh!" He could visualise the whole scene. "But that's only to be expected. Owen has to make allowances for you, his only daughter."

"Perhaps, but I believe it would have been better had he left me out."

"That's ridiculous, Eden, and you know it. See the whole situation from the viewpoint of the lawyer. To leave you out would not only be blatantly unfair but grounds for legal action."

"As though I'd ever bring it." Delma's reactions had so upset her, her control was running thin.

"You mean you're going to allow Delma the whole kit and caboodle?"

"She can have it and Robbie of course. I've got all *I* want."

He sounded impatient. "You're twenty-four years of age, Eden, all sorts of things happen in life. Anyway it's not about money as such, it's the *principle* of the thing. Your father is doing the right thing. He's making amends that were long overdue. Delma should not stand in the way. I've told her that."

Eden spread her hands helplessly. "You mean you've discussed it?"

"She rang me," he answered, a shade grimly.

"She did? When?"

"Somewhere around eleven." He gave her a searching look. "I was due to meet Bruno for a game of golf."

"So she spoke to you the very minute after she stalked off from the table?"

"Eden, I wasn't there," he said reasonably.

"But you *knew* all about it. Were you going to tell me?" She couldn't hide the hurt and conflict in her voice.

"You've perked up, haven't you?" he said, very dryly. "It's Christmas. Surely you're not spoiling for a fight?"

She brushed her hair from her brow distractedly. "You make me believe you're on my side yet you continue as Delma's adviser?"

"Stop it, Eden," he advised, catching her hand momentarily. "I know you're feeling low. Delma wanted a bit of advice and I gave it to her. Plus a few home truths."

"Not before time," she said emotionally, "but you still feel sorry for her?" She had to face the painful truth.

"I know Delma's limitations, Eden. I know your strengths. You're a very understanding, compassionate person."

"Who can also feel anger and disappointment...disillusionment? Does being compassionate mean I have to swallow all these insults?" Her head seemed to be spinning, her blood running hot. She broke off abruptly, ashamed of herself. "Oh, why am I going on like this? I'm sorry. I'll say no more. I have to tell Dad I won't be with him for Christmas. He's not going to like it."

No he won't, Lang thought, with an intimate knowledge of his partner. "It's your decision, Eden," he pointed out. "You must follow your own heart."

Eden nodded, speaking quietly as if deep in the past. "Grandpa was always there for me. He loved my mother best in the world. He adored her. But he loved me, too. He was kindness itself. When anything needed fixing—all sorts of situations—we fixed it together."

"So you must go to him."

She wished she could see his *exact* expression. Loving him so much she was still so unsure of him. But then hadn't she lived with insecurity all her life? "You're not trying to dissuade me?"

"No, I'm not!" His vibrant tones rang. "It so happens I agree with your decision."

"Well that's a surprise." The instant she said it, so dryly, she would have given anything to draw it back. It was a stupid, spontaneous, meaningless remark.

Lang's face tautened. "I'll forget you said that," he said.

There was no time to apologise. She saw all the cars. She saw the big flood-lit house. There was a giant Christmas tree on the broad sweep of the front lawn. Robbie would have loved to have seen all the sparkling lights.

Inside the house the beautifully appointed rooms were filled with people, most of them Eden had already met at the party her father and Delma had given for her. She thought for a sick minute Lara Hansen might be there just to cap the day off, but mercifully there was no sign of her....

It was a strange night. Although Lang stayed with her most of the time the tension between them only seemed to grow. He hadn't come to terms at all with her silly off-the-cuff remark. She had too little opportunity to explain herself. What she did know was she should never say anything so stupid again.

Her father confounded her by being in fine form. Evidently his little spat with Delma hadn't put him off having a bit of fun. For all she knew they had those kinds of spats all the time. Delma was a volatile woman at the best of times. Owen had a fund of really funny big-game fishing stories that kept people laughing. Whenever she came near him he threw his arm around her waist, telling everyone as if they didn't already know from his attitude towards her, he was the proud father of this beautiful young woman. All his friends drank to that. Eden had made an excellent impression. It was when her father started telling people they would see her again Christmas Day, Eden realised she would have to say something that very night. She couldn't allow her father to launch into yet another story about how wonderful it would be to have his newfound daughter with him.

The chance to speak to her father came when a late arrival waved madly at Lang. It was a woman around thirty, looking quite wonderful.

"Excuse me," Lang murmured to her. "I must say hello to Pat. She's been in the States for the past year. You'll have to meet her."

Pat. From the sound of his voice he really liked her. Pat looked a vibrant, full of confidence person.

Eden at her father's shoulder reached out with a gentle touch. "Dad, do you mind if I have a word with you?"

"Mind?" Owen turned to give a wide smile. "What is it, sweetheart? Why so serious? Where's Lang?" He looked away across the room. Lang had never been far from his daughter's side. And that pleased him mightily.

"He's gone to speak to someone called Pat."

"Ah, Patricia Heeler!" Owen, too, looked delighted. "She and Marty have been overseas. It's great they're back. You'll like them. Anyway, what is it you want to say, darling?" Owen put his arm around his daughter's shoulders and drew her towards the relative privacy of the terrace.

Her father seemed so happy for a moment Eden couldn't speak. She felt terribly defensive now she had to tell him she wouldn't be with him Christmas Day.

"Hey, what's this about?" A concerned expression crossed Owen's ruggedly handsome face.

Eden cleared her throat. "Dad, I have to tell you I've made arrangements to spend Christmas with Grandpa."

Owen winced as though she'd driven her high heel into his foot. "You've arranged this?"

Eden nodded quickly. "I've been wanting to tell you, but you were enjoying yourself so much."

Owen looked threatened, then angry. "I can't believe you'd do this to me, sweetheart. Our first Christmas together. Why do you think I'm so happy?" He gestured aggressively as though against some invisible opponent. "I've told everybody…"

Eden lowered her head. "I'm so sorry. I should have spoken earlier."

"You can change your mind," Owen said sharply. "In

fact I expect you to change your mind. For *me*. For *Robbie*. Delma will be disappointed.''

She desperately wanted his approval but she had made her decision. ''I've given this a lot of thought. Grandpa has taken my mother's death terribly hard.'' She looked away from his set expression.

''And I haven't?'' Owen challenged, somehow managing to keep his voice down.

''A father's love is something else again. Grandpa hasn't been able to focus on anything. The blow was too sudden, too destructive. But when I spoke to him he sounded so pleased I wanted to be with him.''

Owen laughed. A harsh discordant sound. ''You don't owe that old man a damned thing.''

''Yes I do!'' Eden made her loyalty plain. ''Grandpa was there for me, Dad. My mother was a ghost you couldn't get rid of. Don't you think I want to be with you and Robbie? I love you.'' Tears pulsed up but she held them back determinedly. ''It's just that I think it would be too cruel to let Grandpa spend Christmas alone. You'll have Delma and Robbie, all your friends around you. He'll have no one. Or at least no one he wants.''

She touched her father's chest, at a spot over his heart. ''Please try to understand.''

But Owen couldn't absorb his tremendous disappointment. ''I'm sorry, Eden, I don't think I can. Why should I feel sorry for your grandfather? He wrecked lives.''

''*Your* life isn't wrecked, Dad,'' she pointed out, very quietly. ''You've had bad times but you've come through them.''

Owen looked over her head. ''I'm not sure I can take this. I know you're a good girl. Very tender-hearted but I think you owe Christmas day to me.''

He left her where she stood.

* * *

It was Lang who found her leaning against the balustrade, staring out into the beautiful tropical garden, illuminated further by a brilliant flash of lightning.

"I saw Owen go in." He took up a position beside her. "By the look on his face you told him you're going to your grandfather?"

"I knew I'd upset him," Eden answered, low-voiced. "It's a very emotional time."

"You could change your mind, I suppose." He looked down at her unhappy expression.

"I won't!" Now she faced him directly, lifting her chin. "Dad has to get used to my making my own decisions. This one is based on love and my own integrity. I don't know how many more years my grandfather has left. He's seventy-five and my mother's death has crippled him."

"Give your father a little time," Lang suggested. "He'll come 'round."

"How many days are left? I intend leaving Christmas Eve. Dad knows, but he's ignoring the fact Delma doesn't really want me."

"The truth is your father is giving Delma time to make a turn-around. In a way she's in shock. They'll reconcile. They always do."

"There you go again." She sighed.

He ran a finger down her cheek. The first vaguely tender gesture of the evening. "I'm looking from the outside in. You wouldn't want your father to end his marriage? There are plenty of women out there ready to snaffle him."

"Of course I don't want him to." Eden was genuinely shocked. "Delma waits on Dad hand and foot. She picks all his clothes. She even lays his outfits out on the bed for him. She runs the house brilliantly. Once I'm out of the way..."

"Things will settle, I know. I'll talk to Owen. You'll have to say good-night to our hosts."

"Of course." She spoke very calmly but she knew she would have to be very careful, very controlled.

* * *

The storm threatened all the way back to the house. Fireworks lit up the sky. Thunder rolled in from the sea. The trees and towering palms were all in motion. Flurries of spent leaves blazed copper in the headlights.

"Where are we going?" she came out of an unhappy fugue to ask. Instead of taking the side road that led to her father's house, Lang had continued along the main road. "I thought you were taking me home."

"What are you going home for?" he asked in a sardonic voice, flicking a glance at her. "To sit in a lonely house?"

"But we're driving into an electrical storm." She stared at the storm. "Where could we go?"

"My place," he answered bluntly. "That's if you don't find it *too* depressing."

He didn't speak again until they pulled into the underground parking lot of his apartment building.

"Frightened?" He helped her out, silver eyes glittering in his dark striking face.

Of what? She didn't answer. Heart pounding. Whatever was going to happen she couldn't stop it. Although she knew perfectly well where Lang lived, she had never visited his apartment. To be alone with him would have been much too demanding.

And now?

They stood side by side in the lift that took them to the penthouse. Neither spoke, though the air was charged with as much electricity as the night air outside. She knew she was on the edge of a precipice; that danger trembled within her. There was something different in Lang's handsome face. He, too, was on the edge as though it had all gone beyond the point where their lives could be changed or reshaped.

He unlocked the door, turned on the lights.

Eden's eyes raced around the large, open-plan room. She saw *him* in the decoration. Confident, masculine, cultured, very stylish with some beautiful artworks here and there to add drama.

"This is wonderful," she said, coughing a little because

her throat was dry and she was over-stimulated. "It speaks of you."

"What does it say?" He took her evening purse from her and set it down on a mahogany console where it rested between two gilt-bronze winged lions.

"You have great taste. You're a very confident man. You love beautiful things."

"It's not a home. It's a retreat," he told her. "I know what I want to build when the time's right. There are some great views from the balcony. We might as well take a look before the storm really sets in."

What was a storm compared to the tumult of desire?

He opened the massive sliding doors that led onto the balcony. The wind straight off the sea was lashing at the fronds of the golden canes that were set in huge ceramic pots, scattering the hanging flower clusters of the two magnificent medinillas that normally would be protected by the roof of the balcony.

Even as they stood there, both exulting in the awesome power of nature, a great flurry of spray with the sting of salt suddenly hit the balcony, rattling the sliding-glass doors with its force.

"Lord!" Immediately Lang's arms came around her, drawing her back. "Damn it's wet your beautiful dress!"

"It doesn't matter." The bodice was clinging to her like a second skin, the tightly budded peaks of her nipples clearly visible, betraying her state of arousal. "Please, it *doesn't*," she repeated when he looked like he didn't believe it. "Anyway the front of your shirt is damp and the shoulders of your jacket." She studied him very briefly. The spray had sheened his tawny skin making it gleam like bronze.

His sculptured mouth twitched. "I dare not say you could take it off. There's a clothes dryer but it looks much too delicate for that."

"A hair dryer?" she asked, inexplicably beginning to shiver.

He thought for a moment. "Yes there is. I rarely use it.

Why don't you come through to the bathroom? I'll leave you in privacy.''

The bathroom was state of the art, the marble that had been used for the floor and the walls and the surrounds of the bath as beautiful as jade.

"You can manage?" he asked. It was unimaginable agony keeping his hands off her. "I can find you a shirt. It should cover you nicely." It was difficult to talk, when he was fighting the hard recklessness in him.

For all the evenness of his tone she must have sensed his desire.

"You can't stay here with me," she whispered.

"No." He barely recognised his own voice, laced as it was with a harshness just short of anger. Back to square one. Was she ever going to trust him?

He left her alone, going in search of something she could wear but when he returned with a blue cotton shirt he hadn't even worn, she was still standing forlornly looking into the mirror. Seeing *nothing* he guessed from the inward intensity of her gaze.

"What is it?" he asked in a low urgent voice.

"I'm sorry." She raised her head to him. Her hair after its recent spraying had turned into a riot of curls and waves. "What do you mean?"

"You. Me. Trust." He made a little sweeping gesture with his hand. She actually jumped.

"Oh for God's sake!" he exclaimed. "I'm leaving. Get your dress off. Put on the shirt. I don't know if you're trembling or shivering or both."

She called after him, wanting to tell him it wasn't he she feared, but herself. Loudly he closed the door on her. She had decided on him. He was everything she had ever wanted. But had he decided on her? That was the monumental question. Her wariness she could see was ingrained.

When she returned to the living room he had shut the sliding-glass doors against the storm and was busy making coffee in the long galley kitchen. She could smell the marvellous aroma.

She blew out a breath, a little nervous at letting him see her in his shirt. He was a big man. Very tall with wide shoulders. The expensive shirt, the cotton so fine it felt like silk, bunched all around her, skimming her knees. She felt incredibly conscious of her woman's body. Her evening dress had a light inbuilt bra, now she was without one. Not that he could possibly notice. Except for the colour and the fineness of the shirt's fabric she might just as well have been dressed in a sack.

When she came into the kitchen to join him he shot her a cool look. "Everything okay?"

She nodded, readjusting a rolled-up sleeve. "After a moment I didn't like to continue using the hair dryer. It was making a watermark. I'll let it dry naturally."

"Well you're welcome to my shirt," he said offhandedly. "Though you look a bit lost in it." Now *that* was a sign of his control! But he was determined to put her at her ease, divided between a feeling of protectiveness and a fierce frustration. He wouldn't want tests like this too often. "Sugar, cream?" he asked sleekly, noting she, too, kept her distance.

"A teaspoon of sugar…"

"…makes the medicine go down," he finished, aiming a smile at her.

For the first time she smiled back, her expression innocent, her blue-violet eyes on his face. "And I think I'll have a little cream."

"Anything with it? We missed supper."

Instantly she was all apologies. "I'm sorry. I've brought you away from your friends."

"Don't be sorry."

Though he only flipped a glance at her it had so much male sensuality in it, it nearly stopped Eden's breath.

Lang loaded the coffee cups onto a small silver tray and gestured to her to precede him into the living room.

"I hope Robbie's not frightened," she said, staring out at the driving rain.

"My bet is Robbie will sleep right through it," he reassured her. "The house is air-conditioned. We all knew about the storm so the shutters will have been closed. Anyway, Maria is there. She's pretty much his nanny."

"I'm glad. I've been worried." Eden sat in an armchair and curled her legs under her.

"Your toes look good enough to eat," he observed laconically, handing her her coffee. She had beautiful limbs. Beautiful hands.

"Dad was so mad at me," she said wistfully. "I wish he could see my side."

"He was looking forward to having you." He took the sofa opposite her, drawing in the desperate loveliness of her. "Don't worry about it."

"I can't help it. I must have the capacity to hurt."

"And be hurt."

"Yes." She bowed her dark curly head. "I never knew the situation with my father's family was going to be so difficult. I guessed Delma wasn't going to greet me with open arms. Not her husband's newfound daughter some twenty years on. But I wasn't prepared for her hostility. It's not going to be happy-ever-after."

He swallowed a mouthful of the hot, fragrant coffee, set the cup down. "Delma will have to work that out. She's not stupid. Blood binds you not only to her husband but to her son. Robbie couldn't have accepted you more readily into his life."

"And I'm so grateful. I suppose we can't have everything, right?"

"The question is what are you going to do next?" He looked at her, unable to hide the desire that was showing in his eyes.

It set off shock waves. Floods of feeling that rushed through Eden, along with her own hungers. "Oh God knows!'' She couldn't hide her vulnerability. ''I've never felt so happy and so unhappy in my life.''

''You know I'm in love with you,'' he said, knowing there was no way he would give her up. ''Obviously that's proving too intimidating?''

His actual admission made the breath back up in her throat. ''Intimidating?''

''You're going to deny it?'' He stared straight at her.

''It's not so surprising is it, Lang?'' she appealed to him. ''You're a very dynamic man. There's such *intensity* in you.''

''So what am I doing wrong?'' he asked sardonically.

''Nothing. You're perfect.''

''Really?'' One black brow shot up. ''Your lack of trust had me nearly seething tonight.''

''I'm sorry. What I said was a stupid off-the-cuff thing. Of course I trust you.''

''Prove it.'' His silver gaze lanced through her.

''How?''

She looked so alarmed he almost expected her to shoot to her feet. ''Do you feel you don't know me well enough to trust me?'' he questioned.

''You don't know *me*, do you?'' she countered.

''I want to.'' His eyes ravished her. ''I want to know every little thing about you. Flesh, bone, mind and heart. Do you think you can ever allow me to do that?''

At his glance such sensation raced through her, her back arched involuntarily. ''What if you tire of me? It happens.''

His voice resonated with the force of his passion. ''You obviously don't know how profoundly you've gotten to me. Do you want to come over here?'' he asked, very slowly. ''*I'm* the one waiting for you.''

Her whole body began to blossom like a flower, petal after petal opening out to the sun.

This was inevitable. She prayed she could handle it.

Her heart pumping wildly she rose to go to him, aware his eyes were tracking her every movement. She had almost reached him when the phone rang so stridently it startled them both. The atmosphere was so intimate, so electric, the sound came like a gunshot.

For a moment Lang contemplated not answering it, if he could speak at all, then he got to his feet, his eyes seeking Eden's as he recognised the voice at the other end.

He listened for a long moment then said, "She's safe with me, Owen."

To Eden's ears it sounded the most wonderful thing that had happened to her.

She stood up, staring at Lang's very serious face. "Is that Dad?"

"He wants to speak to you." Lang held out the phone reassuringly.

Shaking inside, Eden went to take it. "Yes, Dad?"

There was an explosion of apology at the other end. "Just do what you want to do, my darling," Owen said finally. "We'll have plenty of Christmases together."

Eden felt weak with gratitude for her father's change of attitude. He seemed extremely repentant. "Don't think I don't want to spend it with you. I do," she told him emotionally.

"My dearest girl, I understand the bond you share with your grandfather," Owen cut in, remorseful. "I understand and applaud your love and compassion. Lang has suggested to me it might be a fine thing if your grandfather and I could meet sometime."

Eden turned back to look at Lang, an extraordinary light in her blue-violet eyes. "It might go a long way to healing the wounds."

"So then, for you, I'll see what I can do," Owen promised solemnly. "Delma was upset with me as well when I told her. In fact she was very much on your side. I can be pretty awful at times."

"I love you." Eden smiled through a shimmering haze of tears.

"And I love you." Owen's voice was deep with emotion.

"Now I'll hand you back to Lang. In my view my most trusted friend. You can tell me what you think of him later," he laughed. "Be happy, my darling."

"Dad doesn't mind I'm going to see Grandpa," Eden said wonderingly, walking slowly towards Lang as though he was the source of all love and comfort. "He even promised to meet him just as you suggested."

"That's great news, Eden," Lang said. "Both of them will find they're happier."

"I feel like I'm floating," she exclaimed with a sudden rush of joy.

"Me, too," he said, astonishing her. "Come and sit beside me on the sofa. I'll go mad if I don't make love to you. God knows how I haven't so far."

Clearly he was waiting for her next move. She felt a little shy but extraordinarily physical, acutely aware of her woman's body and its power. Love was an expanding force. Hope bloomed inside her like some marvellous vision of the future. "Dad even said Delma took my side for once." She laughed, quite literally light-headed.

"Try understanding a woman!" Lang said dryly. "Delma has her good side. She'll settle down once you're safely married."

"That would be wonderful if I could manage it." Radiance filled her. "Marriage to the right man…"

"Then you'd better not look past me," he warned, looking squarely at her with those silver eyes.

She hadn't been fully expecting it. In fact she hesitated as though she wasn't quite sure what he had said. "When you say things like that, how can I think properly?"

"Do you want me to repeat it?" he asked crisply. His eyes were very brilliant as he looked at her.

"Yes please." Tears glinted though she was smiling.

"Only if you come over here." He held out his hand very purposefully.

She went to him quickly, almost at a run, flinging out her arms so he pulled her down to him in a passionate hug, lifting her like she weighed nothing, settling her across his knees, the full length of her long satiny legs exposed.

"I love you, so help me," he said passionately, tilting back her head. "You're a continual delight to me and when I can't have you a torment. Eyes as blue as morning glories. I knew I'd be saying this to you the moment I laid eyes on you."

"You hated me then." The soft radiance of her smile deepened.

"That's what I told myself," he admitted wryly. "The reasons were very complex. I thought I was a man in control but you dazzled me. Set me on fire. Turned my ordered life upside down. For a time that threw me badly. Potentially you were another trauma. I'd been rubbed raw by the loss of my father and the effort I'd put into saving my family."

Tears welled into Eden's eyes. "And they worship you for it. You're everything to your mother."

"As she is to me. But to get back to you, my true, true love. Weren't you the least little bit attracted to me?"

She stretched to lock her arms around his neck. "Whoever loved that loved not at first sight? Isn't that the way it ought to be?"

"My God, yes!" He laughed with fierce joy, bending his head to look down into cloudless black-lashed eyes that reflected his image and the rare and beautiful depth of feeling that was in her. His breath caught in his throat at the prize he had won. He abandoned himself to triumph, bending his head to kiss her. Deeply, voluptuously, infinitely erotic so her slender arms fluttered helplessly to her sides like moths.

He couldn't stop. Slipping the buttons of his shirt so he could find her sweet, luminous breasts. Fruit in his palms. He could hear the deep, powerful purr of his own heart as his hard-won control vanished. Soon he found her secret centre, warm and glistening. Her very core. His need for her was truly wonderful, truly terrible. His breath was ragged, he couldn't imagine wanting any other woman. Every nerve, every sinew, every drop of blood in him cried out for Eden.

She was helpless in his arms, except her soft crooning was freighted with passion, an answering hunger as old as time.

Finally when he could stand it no longer and the need to consummate their love became too urgent, he gathered her up into his arms, bearing her away to his bedroom.

She lay staring up at him, still wearing his shirt. It fanned away from her lovely slender body that was utterly, ecstatically, female. Her magnolia skin was flushed, her long hair curling a sable halo against the dark ruby silk of one of the cushions that adorned the navy coverlet. She looked so beautiful, so innocently seductive, he felt his heart contract with love and protectiveness. "You're sure, my love?"

At that, her whole body surged upward, her hands clutching at the front of his shirt. "Can't you see I'm longing for you?" Her voice broke as she pressed her soft body against him. "More than anything in the world I want your love."

"No going back?" He leaned forward to kiss her sweet, open mouth.

Love bloomed and swelled, encompassing them both.

An enormous certainty seized her. "I know where I am," Eden whispered as his arms closed strongly around her. "My heart knows. My body knows. I'm home!"

HARLEQUIN®
Romance®

is thrilled to present
a brand-new miniseries
that dares to be different...

TANGO
Fresh & Flirty...
it takes two to tango!

Exuberant, exciting...emotionally exhilarating!

These cutting-edge, highly contemporary stories
capture how women in the 21ˢᵗ century *really*
feel about meeting Mr. Right!

Don't miss:

August:
THE HONEYMOON PRIZE—
Jessica Hart (#3713)

October:
THE FIANCÉ FIX—
Carole Mortimer (#3719)

November:
THE BEDROOM
ASSIGNMENT—
Sophie Weston (#3724)

*And watch for more
TANGO books to come!*

HARLEQUIN®
Makes any time special ®

Visit us at www.eHarlequin.com   HRTANGO

magazine

♥ —————————————————————————— **quizzes**

Is he the one? What kind of lover are you? Visit the **Quizzes** area to find out!

♥ —————————————————————— **recipes for romance**

Get scrumptious meal ideas with our **Recipes for Romance**.

♥ ———————————————————————— **romantic movies**

Peek at the **Romantic Movies** area to find Top 10 Flicks about First Love, ten Supersexy Movies, and more.

♥ ———————————————————————————— **royal romance**

Get the latest scoop on your favorite royals in **Royal Romance**.

♥ —————————————————————————————————— **games**

Check out the **Games** pages to find a ton of interactive romantic fun!

♥ ————————————————————————— **romantic travel**

In need of a romantic rendezvous? Visit the **Romantic Travel** section for articles and guides.

♥ ————————————————————————————— **lovescopes**

Are you two compatible? Click your way to the **Lovescopes** area to find out now!

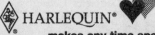

HARLEQUIN® ♥

makes any time special—online...

Visit us online at
www.eHarlequin.com

HINTMAG

COOPER'S CORNER

The latest continuity from Harlequin
Books continues in October 2002 with

STRANGERS WHEN WE MEET
by Marisa Carroll

Check-in: Radio talk-show host Emma Hart thought Twin
Oaks was supposed to be a friendly inn, but fellow guest
Blake Weston sure was grumpy!

Checkout: When both Emma and Blake find their fiancés
cheating on them, they find themselves turning to one
another for support—and comforting hugs quickly turn to
passionate embraces....

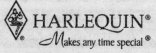

HARLEQUIN®

Makes any time special®

Visit us at www.cooperscorner.com

CC-CNM3